To Whom the Glory?

To Whom the Glory?

CHARLES MACKINNON

A Scottish Chronicle

1935–1945

HURST & BLACKETT

044504

HURST & BLACKETT LTD
3 Fitzroy Square, London W1

An imprint of the Hutchinson Publishing Group

London Melbourne Sydney Auckland
Wellington Johannesburg Cape Town
and agencies throughout the world

First published 1974

Set in Intertype Plantin
Printed in Great Britain by The Anchor Press Ltd
and bound by Wm Brendon & Son Ltd
both of Tiptree, Essex

ISBN 0 09 121600 1

For
KIRSTIN

THE MACINNES FAMILY GENEALOGY

ROBERT MACINNES ('Merchant Bob') (1854–1917) m. 1878 Elizabeth MacKinnon (1857–1922)

(A) CHILDREN OF MERCHANT BOB

ALASDAIR ('Dair')	(1879–1917)	m. 1908 *Norma* Beresford	(1884–1974)
CHARLES	(1882–1938)	m. 1905 *Catriona* MacLeod	(1883–1908)
		m. 1910 *June* Haverford	(1890–1925)
		m. 1928 *Vivienne* de Gauley	(1901–1971)
DONALD	(1883–1915)	died unm.	
KENNETH ('Wee Ken')	(1885–1940)	m. 1906 *Janet* Rutherford	(1888–1940)
ROBERT ('Bobbie')	(1888–1936)	died unm.	

(B) GRANDCHILDREN OF MERCHANT BOB

(1) ALASDAIR'S CHILDREN

ALASDAIR ROBERT ('Alasdair Beg')	(1910–1944)	m. 1934 *Fiona* Campbell of Innisfearn	(1914–
MARY ('May')	(1912–)	m. 1937 Squadron Leader *Robert* Loring, DSO, DFC, AFC, RAF	(1913–1941)
ELIZABETH ('Betty')	(1914–1936)	died unm.	

(2) CHARLES'S CHILDREN

GORDON	(1906–1941)	m. 1932 *Annabelle* Fairfax (U.S.A.)	(1909–1941)
SUSAN	(1912–	m. 1931 Lord *Maurice* Blood, KCMG	(1902–

(3) KENNETH'S CHILDREN

FINVOLA (1907–1970) } died unm.
ALINE IONA ('Leona') (1909–) } m. 1933 Sir *Lauchlan* MacKinnon (1903–1950)
Bt., KCIE, CSI, ICS
('Rajah Sahib')

DOUGAL (1913–) m. 1931 *Elena* Sotomayor y
Perales de Mendoza (1917–)

ANDREW (1916–1941) died unm.

(4) ROBERT'S ILLEGITIMATE CHILD

DEIDRE (1924–)

(C) GREAT-GRANDCHILDREN OF MERCHANT BOB

(i) *Alasdair Beg's Children*
Charles Robert Alasdair (1935–)
('Pal Al')
Frances Mary (1938–)

(ii) *Gordon's Children*
Jean (1936–)
Charles (1937–)

(iii) *Susan's Children*
Vernon Blood (1933–)
Philip Blood (1935–)

(iv) *Leona's Children*
Eve MacKinnon (1935–)
Mary MacKinnon (1936–)

(v) *Dougal's Child*
Torquil Rafael

I

Fiona MacInnes looked out of the car windows at the pouring rain. They were passing through Glenfinnan at the head of Loch Shiel, and Castlemore was only six miles distant. After the brassy heat and the garish colours of Peshawar the chill rain and the subdued greens and blues of the West Highland countryside in March provided a contrast about which she could not quite make up her mind. She had looked forward so eagerly to getting out of India, to turning her back on the dirt and dust, the impassive unsympathetic brown faces, the restricted, shallow, facile society of the English abroad, and everything that was so alien to her whole nature and upbringing.

On this miserable wet afternoon of Friday, 22nd March 1935, the contrast was brought home with a vengeance. Dark clouds lowered on the horizon, water dripped from trees, Loch Shiel was a dull leaden colour, and the stone figure of Prince Charlie looked dejected and forlorn on its tall column. She was surprised that there had been no one at Fort William to meet her, only the chauffeur whom she did not remember having seen before, with a note from Norma. It was a brief note of apology, simply saying she was sorry she could not come. If her mother-in-law could not come, Fiona wondered, why could not her sister-in-law, Betty? Betty was twenty and lived at home. It was an odd sort of welcome back after almost a year away. There had been no real time to get to know her new family, because less than a month after their marriage she and Alasdair Beg had sailed for India with the regiment.

She shivered a little and was uncomfortably aware of her apprehension. Three months ago she had been overjoyed when the doctor had told Alasdair and her that she must return to Britain or he would not be responsible for her. The constant sickness, for which no cause had been discovered, had weakened her and left her depressed and listless. Their first Christmas together had not been a happy one, and she would be spending her first wedding anniversary apart from him, living with his family at Castlemore. She wished she could go home to Castle Fearn, on the shores of Loch Awe, but in the short time she had been away her father had died, her elder brother had succeeded to the castle and the depleted bank balance, and had married. At Castlemore, on the other hand, they were expecting her. One day she would be its mistress. She supposed that technically she was already its mistress as Alasdair's father was dead. On the other hand Norma, his widow, was very much in charge of the situation. Fiona sighed and hoped it would all turn out well. She was only twenty, and sometimes life overwhelmed her.

When she saw little Loch Eilt on her left, her spirits revived somewhat. She recalled Castlemore as she had seen it last, gracious, beautiful, overlooking the loch. They were almost home. She leaned forwards in her seat and stared ahead. She saw the line of tall firs running down to the edge of the road which formed the eastern boundary of the grounds. A few moments later they turned in through the big stone gateposts whose wrought-iron gates were open, and drove along the wide gravelled drive between the evergreen trees which lined it. One final turn to the left and there stood the house, on their right, with its big portico supported on four beautiful fluted columns, and the curious dome on the roof behind it. She could see the broad lawns, the summer house and the fountain, and all around them the hills reared up to the sky. Even in the driving rain and the dull light Castlemore retained its beauty and its dignity.

Inglis, the new chauffeur, held open the car door for her, and she ran quickly up the steps to the doors. The large, heavy wooden double doors were open, and as she reached the top the glass-fronted inner door opened also and she saw her mother-in-law smiling at her.

'Fiona.' Norma held out her arms in an embrace.

Fiona hugged her gingerly. 'I'm a bit wet,' she apologized.

'Only damp, my dear. Give your coat to Fraser and come and warm yourself by the fire.' Norma turned to the footman. 'Help Inglis with Mistress Fiona's luggage, Fraser, then ask Jean to unpack for her please. This way, Fiona.'

She led the way into what had once been the smoking room. It was refurnished now and was an extremely beautiful sitting room. A big fire blazed in the fireplace and two standard lamps cast a warm glow. Norma rang a bell and turned to her daughter-in-law.

'Come over here by the fire and let me look at you. You're pale. I expected you to be sunburned.'

'I haven't been very well. I didn't go out much during the last few months.'

'Of course not. How silly of me.' The parlourmaid entered. 'Ipla, would you bring tea now, please.'

'Yes, ma'am.'

Suddenly Fiona's fears and uncertainties vanished. Here, in the safety and comfort of the big house with its ordered and orderly life, she was immediately at home. She felt safe and sheltered. She smiled at Norma, a smile which transfigured her face. Norma realized with surprise that Alasdair's wife was beautiful. That was strange, for she had not remembered her as beautiful at all, just as being tall and willowy with nice long fair hair.

'Tell me everything,' Norma commanded. 'How was the journey?'

'Not very pleasant, especially the last part through the

Bay of Biscay and the English Channel. There were storms, but luckily I don't suffer from seasickness.'

'What about the other sickness?'

'It stopped the day after we sailed from Bombay.'

'How odd. Nobody knew what it was?'

'No,' Fiona said. 'Every morning at about seven I would be sick, for perhaps an hour, till there was nothing left. It was awful.'

'It sounds it. Just in the mornings?'

'Mostly, though sometimes during the night. Of course at first I jumped to the obvious conclusion, but after a month or two it became clear it wasn't that.'

'How do you feel now?'

'Tired,' Fiona smiled, 'but I'll be all right.'

'Fresh air and good food will work wonders. No more India for you, young lady. I suppose there is no chance of Alasdair coming home soon, is there?'

'None,' Fiona answered sadly. 'The regiment is supposed to be out there for five years.'

'Heaven help us. That won't do at all.'

The two women smiled. Norma was fifty, but it was difficult for anyone to guess her age, for there was a timeless look about her. She was slim and upright and had a remarkably good figure. She never wore any make-up other than a little powder, which perhaps was why she had such a fine complexion. She opened a box of cigarettes and held it out, but Fiona shook her head. Norma laughed.

'I started it years ago, and now I enjoy it too much to want to give it up. I can remember when it was considered very daring and not very nice for women to smoke, even in the privacy of the house. My mother-in-law wouldn't permit smoking in the dining room or the drawing room or any of the bedrooms.'

Ipla returned with a trolley and for a few minutes Norma was busy pouring tea and offering sandwiches and scones.

'Well,' she said at length, 'what's the news from India? How is Alasdair?'

'He's very well. He loves it. They go off on patrols, you know, chasing tribesmen. It's just as well I left because he was going to Landi Kotal, which is a sort of forward camp right at the entrance to the Khyber Pass. Women aren't allowed there.'

'It doesn't sound like much of a life for you,' Norma said sympathetically, 'but I can well believe Alasdair enjoys it. He's exactly like his father. Luckily Dair was never sent to India after we were married. He'd been out there just before I met him.'

'It's no place for women,' Fiona told her. 'It's a man's world. I daresay some women like it, the sort who never had a servant in their lives before and who find pleasure in interminable games of bridge with other wives at the club. I thought it was ghastly.'

Norma nodded. She had feared as much. She didn't blame Fiona at all. She herself would have reacted in exactly the same way.

'Did you see Leona and her husband?' she asked.

Fiona nodded. Leona was Alasdair's cousin, married to Sir Lauchlan MacKinnon of the Indian Civil Service. Wee Ken, Leona's father, who lived about thirty miles away at Ardclune House, had nicknamed Sir Lauchlan 'Rajah Sahib'. Rajah Sahib, who had succeeded some years back to his father's baronetcy, was now a very young and promising District Commissioner at Sialkot.

'We met them very briefly in Lahore,' she said to Norma. 'We hoped they might manage to come to Peshawar, but the visit fell through.'

'Nevertheless you saw them? They're well?'

'Yes, they're very well. Leona's baby is due in April, as I expect you know. Rajah Sahib got the C.S.I. in the New Year's Honours.'

'That's good, isn't it? He's only in his thirties.'

'Very good,' Fiona agreed. 'Most unusual in fact. He was only given his District quite recently, and the Star of India is senior to the Order of the Indian Empire. They must think highly of him in Delhi. Somebody said he's a friend of the Viceroy, but I don't know if it's true.'

'I shouldn't think so,' Norma retorted. 'That's just gossip. None of his family ever had anything to do with India. They've lived in Arisaig for donkey's years and they've got no influence at all. If Rajah Sahib is getting ahead it's because of merit.'

Fiona nodded and smiled.

'I'm sorry I couldn't come to the station to meet you,' Norma remarked, changing the subject without warning. 'You must have thought me very rude sending Inglis with a note like that.'

'I wondered if something was wrong.'

'Something is. It's Betty.'

'She's ill?' Fiona asked.

'She has been in bed for the past week. She's upstairs in her room now.'

'What's the trouble?' Fiona asked anxiously. She had been intending to ask about Betty, but had assumed that she was out.

'I don't know. Dr Martin from Corpach has been to see her twice and I think he's as puzzled as I am. She has a pain in her head.'

'A headache?'

'A sort of headache but it's at the back of her head. It makes her feel sick and dizzy. She's going to Inverness on Monday for an X-ray.'

'I'm sorry. I've come home at an awkward time, haven't I?'

'My dear, you're welcome. You must believe that. It will be good for me to have you here. What with Alasdair away and May in Hereford, then Betty's being off-colour since before Christmas, it hasn't been exactly gay.

14

I visit Ken and Janet at Ardclune about once a fortnight.'

'How is Andrew? He's the one who's an idiot, isn't he?' Fiona asked.

'Yes, their youngest. He's the only one left at Ardclune, you know. Finvola has been in London for the past seven years – or somewhere near London anyway – Leona is in India and Dougal is in Seville. Times have changed since the war.' She made a gesture towards the teapot as she spoke.

'How do you mean?' Fiona asked, holding out her cup for more tea.

'There used to be so many of us, but now Grunaglack is empty. It was rented out for several years but there's been nobody there since Charles went to Paris. Ken and Janet are tied down at Ardclune with Andrew, and I'm alone here with my own invalid.'

'What about Alasdair's other uncle, Bobbie?'

'Bobbie is doing splendidly in Edinburgh. Of course I don't see him as often as I would like. I thought of going to visit them this summer, if there's time and if Betty's health allows me to get away for a few days.'

'I don't know much about Bobbie,' Fiona said hesitantly. 'Only little bits that Alasdair has let drop. He was in prison, wasn't he?'

'Twice, but the second time he was innocent. He's a changed man now. I'm very proud to know Bobbie.'

Fiona thought that that was a strange thing for Norma to say, but she did not comment on it. After tea she went upstairs to wash and change out of her travelling clothes. She was surprised to find herself in what was obviously the main bedroom, an enormous room at the front of the house above the portico, looking south-west across the loch. It had its own dressing room and two beautiful large single beds, almost large enough to be doubles. Then she recalled from previous visits that Norma slept in what had always been her husband's bedroom from childhood onwards, a big airy room in the southern corner of the building. Norma had never troubled to move out, apparently preferring it, like her husband.

She saw that Norma's maid had unpacked everything for her and put it away tidily. She was looking in the huge mahogany wardrobe, wondering what to wear, when someone tapped on the door and came in. It was Jean, the lady's maid.

'Mistress MacInnes sent me to see if I can help you, madam,' the girl said respectfully.

'No thanks,' Fiona stammered. 'I'd rather manage by myself.'

'Very good, madam. If there is anything you need, please ring.'

She went out and Fiona smiled at herself. She hated ladies' maids, hated being fussed over. Her room was a place to be private, not to be shared with a servant. She went to the nearest bathroom and had a good soak in a hot bath, which made her feel much better. She put on a scarlet woollen dress, which went well with her very fair hair, and a gold necklace and a gold brooch. The effect was pleasing. Then she went along the corridor to Norma's room, and knocked.

'Come in,' Norma called, and Fiona went inside.

'Hullo, Fiona. You look very nice.'

'I haven't worn this dress for ages.'

'I suppose you didn't get any chance in India, did you? Too hot?'

The question surprised Fiona, who overlooked the fact that Norma had never been out of Britain and rarely out of Scotland.

'As a matter of fact it can be very cold in Peshawar in the winter and sometimes there's snow,' she laughed. 'It isn't hot all the time, although I always remember it most as a hot, dusty and incredibly dirty place.'

'I know when Leona writes she always seems to say how nice and warm it is out there.'

'I came to ask if I could see Betty,' Fiona ventured, de-

16

ciding that it was profitless to pursue the topic of the Indian climate which varied enormously from place to place as well as from time to time.

'Yes of course. I'll take you to her. I think she's awake.'

Norma got up from her dressing table and led the way past the master bedroom to the room next to it, adjoining the nursery. Originally it had been Charles's room, then Bobbie's, and now Betty had it. They went inside. Betty, who was sitting up in bed, turned expectantly and stared at Fiona.

'Darling, this is Alasdair Beg's wife, Fiona. You remember her, don't you?'

Betty frowned. 'I think so. Hullo Fiona.'

'Hullo Betty. How are you tonight?'

'Much better. My head doesn't hurt.'

As she spoke both hands were unconsciously plucking nervously at the bedclothes. She was pale and drawn with deep shadows under her eyes. Fiona thought that she looked dreadfully ill.

'Fiona's just come back from India.'

'Have you?' Betty spoke without much interest, and Fiona contented herself with a nod.

'Is there anything I can get you darling?' Norma asked.

'No thanks.'

'What about something to read?'

'It hurts my eyes.' Betty was now becoming petulant. 'I'll be all right if I'm left alone.'

'I see. Well, we'll go down and we'll both see you later. Dinner won't be long.'

'Good. I'm hungry.'

When they were outside in the corridor, Fiona said,

'At least she seems to eat. That's a good sign, isn't it?'

'No,' Norma shook her head. 'She looks forward to meals, but when she gets them she eats hardly anything. She simply nibbles.' She stopped and turned to face Fiona. 'What makes it worse is that somehow I've never been able to get close to Betty. She was always a funny child, living in a world of her own. Sometimes she was like a stranger. Now that she is ill she is even more like someone I don't know.' She shrugged and for a moment her shoulders drooped. Fiona felt a sudden surge of sympathy towards the older woman and put an arm round her waist. Norma was taken aback momentarily, and then she smiled at the girl.

'I'm glad you've come home. Let's hope Alasdair will follow soon,' she said gently, and together they went downstairs.

At the beginning of April Fiona knew that her suspicions were correct – she was having a baby. She consulted Norma who suggested she see Dr Archibald Martin of Corpach, now the 'family doctor' at both Castlemore and Ardclune House. Dr Martin drove over the following afternoon and confirmed the diagnosis. A child was due, some time in September. While he was at the house he saw Betty, but there was nothing he could do to help except give her drugs. The X-rays had shown a deep-seated brain tumour. A whole series of X-ray plates had been sent to a specialist in Edinburgh, who had given it as his opinion that it would be fatal to attempt to operate. Betty, aged twenty, was condemned to death.

The effect of this dreadful news on Norma had not been apparent immediately. Norma was accustomed to misfortune in various guises, and accustomed to remaining calm in a crisis. She had shed her tears privately, in the middle of the night, but slowly she began to seek out Fiona, so that she was rarely away from the younger woman. Fiona did not mind at all. She had fallen naturally into her place as the daughter of the house. She belonged at Castlemore and was happy in Norma's company.

As she sat writing to Alasdair Beg to tell him the news about the baby, she paused and frowned. It occurred to her that she did not really miss him very much, not nearly as much as she had just written. Why was this?

The question plagued her all evening. Alasdair adored her, and made it plain in every possible way. It was really flattering to have a husband so much in love. He was kind to her and considerate. He drank very little, had given up smoking altogether because he considered it affected his fitness, never gambled – not even at whist, steadfastly refusing to play for money, although he had plenty to play with, and certainly he never looked at another woman. Indeed, apart from his almost irrational love for the Army, he was a model husband. He was handsome, athletic, and looked simply marvellous in uniform. Other women in India had envied Lieutenant MacInnes's wife, and with good reason. Why, then, was she so content to be separated from him like this?

She dismissed the matter from her mind, and when she had finished writing to Alasdair she wrote to her mother and to her brother, both at Castle Fearn, telling them the news. She would visit them this summer, possibly when Norma went to Edinburgh. She was looking forward to seeing her home again. It was not nearly as nice as Castlemore, but as a child she had loved it, with its innumerable nooks and crannies, its hidden corners and the worn steps in its old turrets. Now that she was older she realised just how much her mother had had to contend with – old castles seldom make satisfactory homes unless the owners have fortunes to spend on modernization. Her father, Colin Campbell of Innisfearn, had owned a half-share in a sugar plantation which eventually had fought a losing battle against a big combine and had been bought out. Fortunately his elder son was a qualified solicitor as all he had inherited after estate duties was a mere fifty thousand pounds. Fiona and her younger brother, Islay, had received ten thousand each. A century ago the family had had ten thousand a year from its sugar! More, in a good year.

On a fine morning several days later Inglis drove them the thirty miles to Ardclune, the old house two miles out of Onich, overlooking Loch Linnhe and surrounded by a small forest of trees. Wee Ken, in his fiftieth year, still used a stick as a result of wounds he had received as an Observer in the Royal Flying Corps. He wore a faded kilt and a thick tweed jacket, and he had the same jaunty smile which Fiona remembered. He made them welcome, and his old basset hound, Jamie the Saxt, trotted round in circles wagging his tail with delight.

'So this is Fiona. A beautiful girl with a beautiful name,' Ken said, kissing her cheek. 'I'm glad to see you again, Fiona. Come along and meet my wife Janet. She's fussing about in the kitchen. Anyone would think we'd never had a visitor before.'

'What a liar you are, Ken,' a cool voice said from the end of the passage, and they saw Janet smiling at them. 'Come inside, Norma. Hullo, Fiona. What's your news?'

They followed into a rather shabby but very comfortable big old room, and sat down around a huge log fire which gave off the smell of peats. Fiona saw a big wooden box full of peats in the corner, and sniffed appreciatively.

'We've got our own news today, haven't we, darling?' Ken said to Janet as he poured sherry.

'Yes, a letter from India. Leona had her baby on the first of the month, a girl. They're calling her Eve.'

'I'm so glad,' Norma said. 'How are they? All right?'

'Yes, I think so,' Janet answered, taking her glass from Kenneth. 'Rajah Sahib says the doctor isn't too happy about Leona having any more children, but we'll know more about that later.'

They discussed the family news for a time. Wee Ken had heard from Charles in Paris. He talked vaguely about returning to Grunaglack, but in Wee Ken's opinion it was just talk. Charles's wives had always led him a dance and his third one. Vivienne, nineteen years younger than he, was no exception. Charles's financial setbacks did not amuse Vivienne, who had unashamedly married him for his money.

'I never know whether or not to feel sorry for Charles,' Ken mused aloud. 'He's a pathetic figure in my eyes but I have an uncomfortable feeling that he's happy the way he is. If so, it doesn't matter what I or anyone else thinks of him, does it?'

There was no answer to that. Gordon, Charles's son, was now back in Richmond, Virginia, with his wife Annabelle. Gordon seemed to be very much the apple of his father-in-law's eye and Gideon Fairfax was the President of the vast Fairfax Corporation. In the family's opinion Gordon was a success. Nobody ever actually mentioned money, except when discussing the stock markets, but the MacInneses were all sensitive to the importance of money. Even Wee Ken, with his well-developed feeling for the ridiculous, spoke approvingly of Gordon, not because he knew anything at all about Gordon's private life, his happiness or lack of it, but because he had 'done well for himself'. Susan, Charles's other child, was still in Rome with her diplomat husband, Lord Maurice Blood, a younger son of the Marquess of Minchinhampton. They had one son, Vernon, and now another child was on the way.

The arrival of children was important to the family. Children meant continuity, succession, the perpetuation of the tribe.

'What are you going to call yours when it arrives, Fiona?' Janet asked with interest.

'If it's a boy, Charles Robert Alasdair.'

'He couldn't be more of a MacInnes than that,' Wee Ken chuckled, 'and a very diplomatic choice of names too – Charles after the General, Robert after Merchant Bob, and Alasdair after his father and grandfather. Four generations in one go, eh?'

Fiona smiled. 'I had no choice,' she confessed easily. 'Alasdair laid down the law a long time ago.'

'What if it's a girl?' Norma asked.

'We haven't decided – Alasdair will leave it to me.'

There was a little silence. That last remark had had a capricious ring about it which jarred somewhat. Fiona smiled at them blandly. She had no intention of discussing the matter with anyone. In her lifetime very few decisions had been left to her – it had never really been necessary for her to make decisions – and she treasured this particular right. Indeed it was a girl she wanted, although she was far too intelligent to hint at this revolutionary outlook. Votes for women were still regarded as a bit of a joke at Castlemore and Ardclune, and sons were far more important than daughters. If women felt any special tenderness towards their daughters, the fact was never mentioned.

They went on to talk about Norma's second child, May, now a librarian in Hereford. Nobody had really understood why May found it necessary to pursue her career in England. She had started off in Inverness, and if she had wanted a change there were places like Aberdeen and Edinburgh without crossing the border. Despite all of which, May was obviously very happy. She had a cottage in a village called Weobley, a small saloon car for travelling, and her letters were mostly about books. She was a dedicated bibliophile. Dougal, the elder of Wee Ken's two sons, was settled in Seville, working in his father-in-law's business, exactly like Gordon, except that Don Jaime Sotomayor y Perales de Mendoza was a hidalgo, a Spanish aristocrat, and possessed a modest fortune in the form of vineyards. Apparently Dougal was responsible for the sales of the Mendoza wines.

'How is Finvola?' asked Fiona, wondering why her name had not cropped up. Finvola was the eldest of Wee Ken's four children, now twenty-eight and working in England, near London. She was some sort of secretary, so far as Fiona could recall.

'She's all right,' Janet said shortly. 'She doesn't correspond much.'

'What's she doing now?' Fiona asked brightly.

'We're not quite sure. Some sort of charitable work I believe.'

'I thought she was a private secretary.'

'So did we,' Wee Ken agreed with a shrug, 'but her latest letter says that she likes her new job and that charitable work is very rewarding – and that's literally all. You'll find out yourself, one day, Fiona, that children can be very infuriating.'

'She should come home,' Janet muttered, plainly upset by the mention of Finvola.

It was not till much later on, after lunch and tea when they were driving back to Castlemore, that Fiona had a chance to ask Norma about Finvola. Norma gave a little sigh.

'It's not a very happy story. Finvola has always been a trial to her parents, especially to Janet. It's as though she positively dislikes her mother. One doesn't ask questions of course, and I don't know what may have taken place at Ardclune, but Janet isn't a bad mother. It's something inexplicable. I told you that Betty often seems like a stranger to me, that I can't get close to her – well, with Finvola and Janet it's much worse. Finvola can be quite unpleasant. I feel sorry for Janet, because she was so happy when the children were young – even Andrew's affliction never daunted her. Now Finvola is in England, Leona is out in India and Dougal is settled in Spain.'

'Nobody mentioned Andrew and I didn't like to ask. How is he?'

'Nobody mentions him, my dear. It's too tragic. He has to have a full-time nurse. He can't wash and is incontinent.'

'Oh dear,' Fiona sympathized.

'He doesn't recognize them. He really ought to be in an institution, but Ken can't bear the thought of sending him away. I'm afraid Andrew just isn't mentioned.'

'I'm surprised Kenneth is so cheerful,' Fiona remarked.

'He can see the bright side of any situation. He's wonderful with Janet. If it weren't for him, I think she'd lose her sanity. It's too bad of Finvola,' Norma concluded a trifle crossly. 'She ought to consider her parents more and what they have to put up with where Andrew is concerned. A little bit of love and kindness from Finvola would make all the difference in that house, believe me.'

Fiona was silent for the rest of the journey. She had never realized how much unhappiness there was below the surface at Ardclune. Her impression of Wee Ken had been of someone bubbling over with fun and good humour, and Janet had seemed so self-contained and confident, a strong personality. It showed how little one really could judge by appearances.

Despite the double tragedies of the dying Betty and the idiot Andrew, the tentacles of the family had quickly drawn Fiona into its close circle. This was largely Norma's doing. Her relationship with Fiona was infinitely complex. She was a mother to the younger woman, at the same time a friend whose age counted for nothing, and combined with this Norma needed Fiona's comfort and strength to help her bear her own burden.

They were busy in the evenings knitting and crocheting things for the baby, and they shopped in Fort William and Inverness for an expensive and extensive layette. The birth of the baby was of paramount importance to Norma. Charles's daughter Susan had already provided him with a grandson and another baby was due. Ken had two grandchildren – Dougal's son and Leona's new daughter. Only the main branch of the family, at Castlemore House, was without an heir. Just as Fiona was secretly hoping for a daughter, Norma was secretly certain it would be a son, a boy to carry on the tradition started by General Charles. It had missed a generation with Merchant Bob, but her own beloved Dair, and her son Alasdair Beg had pursued Army careers. Alasdair's son would do the same.

Norma hoped that Alasdair Beg and Fiona would have

lots of sons. She wanted to be sure of the future of Castlemore, to be certain that it would never lack an heir. She loved the house and the family more than anything in the world. It was a source of regret to her that she and Dair had only had one son, instead of the five fine sons of Merchant Bob and his wife Elizabeth. It was up to Alasdair Beg and Fiona to put things right.

In June, Norma went to Edinburgh to see her brother-in-law, Bobbie, and Alison Mathieson with whom he lived, unable to marry because Alison's dissolute husband took a fiendish delight in refusing her a divorce. They had a child, a lovely girl called Deirdre. Norma looked forward to the visit. Betty was neither better nor worse, and Fiona had changed her mind about going to Castle Fearn to visit her own family, so would be at Castlemore in case of any crisis. She had suddenly become very big with the child she was carrying and was greatly embarrassed. She no longer wanted to leave the house. She, who was so erect and slim, hated her figure and hated to be seen by anyone other than Norma and the servants.

August presented its own problem, for Fiona's twenty-first birthday was on the 14th of the month.

'I don't know what we can do,' Norma complained one evening after dinner.

'Nothing please,' Fiona laughed. 'I'm not a girl. I'm married and practically a mother. Birthdays don't mean anything any more.'

'Goodness, anyone would think you were over fifty to listen to you. It's awkward with Alasdair in India and you not wanting to see anyone.'

'Please, Norma, forget about my birthday. You can get me a nice chocolate gateau for tea, and that will do.'

There was no party for Fiona, who in truth did not mind at all. She felt very grown-up, now that she was carrying the baby, and superior to such things as birthdays. Wee Ken and Janet made one of their infrequent forays from Ardclune and arrived after lunch, bringing gifts. Alasdair, in India, was at a distinct disadvantage when it came to his wife's twenty-first, but he had sent her a cheque for £500. Norma bought her a lovely sapphire and diamond necklace, and Wee Ken and Janet brought a beautiful antique dressing-table set, silver-backed brushes, mirror and tray, also a silver brooch. There were presents in the post from her mother and brothers at Castle Fearn as well. Fiona was thrilled by it all, and Norma marvelled, for to her it was a poor apology for a birthday, never mind a twenty-first birthday.

They sat down to dinner by themselves, just the two of them. The meal was exactly what Fiona would have ordered had it been left to her – a rich lobster bisque, stuffed capon, and an elaborate trifle. They had some Drambuie with their coffee afterwards and Fiona sighed with content.

'What a lovely day,' she said, 'and what a lovely meal, Norma. I feel delightfully spoiled.'

'That's ridiculous. It was nothing.'

'No, you're wrong, it was . . . I don't know. I can't put it into words. I feel happy, so happy that I could burst. Of course,' she added with a laugh, 'that's probably because I made a pig of myself at dinner.'

'You're not difficult to please, are you?' Norma remarked.

'I'd be very ungrateful if I weren't pleased with life.'

'Your being here has made a big difference to me. I keep thinking what it would have been like if you hadn't been ill in India and forced to come home.'

Fiona nodded slowly. Her homecoming was indeed providential. It would have been awful for Norma alone in the house with a dying daughter.

'Poor you,' she said with sympathy.

Norma shook her head and smiled.

'Life has its ups and downs. I've learned that it helps to count your blessings when things look black. Anyway,

I've nothing to grumble about. Mine has been a good life, and it isn't over by any means.'

Almost three weeks later, on Tuesday 3rd September, the baby was born in the afternoon – a plump lusty boy. Norma, holding him in her arms while he screamed red-faced and the doctor attended to Fiona, smiled to herself. She had always known it would be a boy, another Alas-dair.

'Welcome to Castlemore,' she whispered to the scream-ing child.

2

Afterwards it always seemed to Fiona that during those first two years at Castlemore people were either dying or being born. A matter of days after her own baby was born in September 1935, they heard that Susan and Maurice Blood had had a second son, whom they named Philip. He had been born in Rome, in an expensive nursing home much patronized by the Diplomatic Corps, and being Susan's naturally he arrived dead on time, hardly ever cried and was no trouble to anyone. Susan managed everything excellently, including her offspring.

More awkward than her own twenty-first birthday and infinitely more harrowing was that of Betty, who lingered on in her upstairs room. She was twenty-one on the 8th of December, and like Christmas itself her birthday was a sad occasion. She survived into the New Year, and died on the 1st of February 1936, only a few days after the death of King George V.

They heard from Edinburgh that Alison Mathieson's

husband, Douglas Scott Douglas, had at last drunk himself to death, but this good news, which made Alison free to marry Bobbie, was offset by the fact that Alison was ill. This was followed by a cable from the U.S.A. that Gordon and Annabelle had finally had a child, a girl named Jean, born on the 17th February.

On the 3rd of March the cruel blow fell. Alison died in Edinburgh, of some sort of influenza bug according to the doctor. A broken-hearted Bobbie telephoned Castlemore. Norma, Kenneth and Janet all went to Edinburgh for the funeral. Fiona had to remain at home because she herself had a streaming cold.

Norma was subdued on her return from Edinburgh. Bobbie had seemed to disintegrate before their eyes. He had grown old and haggard overnight and had gone to bed immediately after the funeral, tired of a life which had momentarily become meaningless. The eleven-year-old Deirdre, who worshipped her father, was looking after him.

'Just think of it,' Norma told Fiona, 'all those years living together as man and wife, never free to marry because of that wretched drunken husband of hers, then, just when the horrible man dies, she has to go too. I've never seen anyone so completely beaten by life as Bobbie. Thank God he's got Deirdre, or I'd worry about his mind. I really would.'

'It's terrible,' Fiona sympathized, 'enough to drive anyone mad.'

Fate had not finished its heartless jesting. Nineteen days after his wife's death, when he had pulled himself together and was planning a new life with Deirdre, Bobbie MacInnes was involved in a car accident on the main road from Edinburgh to Glasgow, and killed instantly.

This time Norma returned to Castlemore with a white-faced, saucer-eyed child. At first it seemed that Deirdre had no real idea of where she was. She moved about the house in a daze, did not speak unless spoken to and then gave short direct answers, and picked at her food without interest.

Norma had decided to send her to a day school in Fort William for at least a year. In due course she could go to Miss Weir's Academy in Perth where most of the Mac-Innes girls were sent, but not yet. In the meantime Deirdre was at home. Dr Martin had recommended a month's rest before she went to school, which would take them up to the Easter holidays in mid-April.

A day cot had been put up in the library, next to the sitting room, and there Charles Robert Alasdair spent a good deal of his days when he couldn't be outside in his pram. Fiona had taken to referring to the baby as 'my pal Al', and Pal Al became his nickname from then on. One morning Fiona found Deirdre in the library, bent over the cot. The baby was gurgling as he clung to one of the girl's fingers.

'Hullo, Deirdre.'

'Hullo, Aunt Fiona.'

'I'm not an aunt,' Fiona laughed.

'Aren't you?' Deirdre displayed unaccustomed interest. 'What are you then?'

'I'm your cousin by marriage.'

'Really? You're so old.'

'Now you're putting me in my place. I'm only twenty-one.'

'Are you honestly? I'm eleven but I'll be twelve this year. I thought you were much older.'

Fiona concealed a wry smile. This was not her day for being flattered.

'Pal Al likes you,' she remarked.

'Why do you call him Pal Al?'

'It's a complicated story. His grandfather's name was Alasdair. He was a soldier, very brave.'

'I've heard of him. They called him Dair.'

'That's right. He was your father's brother.' She paused, horrified at her thoughtlessness, but Deirdre was looking at her expectantly. 'Well,' Fiona went on hurriedly, 'he had a son, also called Alasdair – Alasdair Robert. They call him Alasdair Beg, which means little Alasdair. He's my husband.'

'That's two Alasdairs.'

'Three. Pal Al's name is Charles Robert Alasdair.'

'Why are they all called Alasdair?'

'I don't know, but maybe because we're all terribly proud of Dair.'

'Daddy said the Germans killed him.'

'That's right. There was a war you see.'

'Where's your husband?' Deirdre asked, a little lost in this genealogical tangle.

'He's in India, in the Army.'

'Why is he in India? Why doesn't he live here?'

'In the Army you have to go where you're sent. He was sent to India nearly two years ago.'

'Didn't you want to go too?'

'I did, but I was ill and the doctor said I should come home, so here I am, waiting.'

'That doesn't sound much fun.'

'It isn't,' Fiona agreed, laughing.

'Aunt Norma is a real aunt, isn't she?'

'Yes she is.'

'I thought so. Is Pal Al my cousin too?'

'You're his first cousin once removed.'

'I am?' Deirdre stared. 'What's that?'

'You do ask awkward questions. You and Alasdair Beg, my husband, are first cousins. The baby is one generation removed from you, so you're first cousins once removed. Now, if you have a little boy, he'd be Pal Al's second cousin.'

'I don't understand at all.'

'I don't blame you,' Fiona agreed. 'You really need a diagram, and anyway why bother?'

Deirdre nodded. That sounded very sensible. She began to like this cousin rather more.

'What do I call you?' she asked. 'I mean, I was going to call you Aunt Fiona.'

'Just call me Fiona.'

'But you're grown up!'

'You're almost grown up too, aren't you?'

'Won't I get into trouble? What would Aunt Norma say?'

'I'll tell her, shall I? Then she'll know it's all right.'

'Thank you.'

'When Pal Al here is asleep after lunch, would you like to go into Fort William? I could drive us over in the car, just the two of us.'

'What for?'

'I thought you might like to buy some sweets, or comics.'

'I haven't got any money.'

'That's all right, I've got plenty. We'll have to see about pocket money for you. We could have tea there. There's rather a nice place I know where they have lovely cakes.'

'That sounds fun.'

'It makes a change. Shall we do that?'

'Yes please,' Deirdre agreed eagerly.

Fiona told Norma who nodded approval. She had hoped they would make friends. She felt she herself was too much older than Deirdre to be a real companion to the child. They set out after lunch in the little Austin saloon which had been bought two years earlier for Betty when she had passed her driving test. The car had barely been used – it had less than ten thousand miles on the clock – and Norma had told Fiona to make full use of it. This suited Fiona very well as she would have hesitated to drive the big old-fashioned Rolls-Royce even if permitted. That was better left to the professional ministrations of Inglis.

Fiona was surprised how much pleasure she derived from watching Deirdre enjoy herself. For the first time

31

the girl seemed completely relaxed and natural. She was thrilled when Fiona bought her a leather purse and put ten shillings in loose change into it before giving it to her.

'You'll need that,' she said. 'I've spoken to your Aunt Norma, and you're to have two shillings a week pocket money, which you'll get every Saturday. This is just something to start you off.'

'Golly.' Deirdre was impressed. Two shillings was a great deal of money. She thought of all the things she could buy with it. It was sixpence more than her father had given her.

After their shopping they had tea together and drove back to Castlemore.

'Is driving easy?' Deirdre asked.

'Yes, quite easy. When you're seventeen you can sit a driving test and if you pass you get a licence.'

'I'd like to do that.'

'I'll teach you if you like – not now, but later on when you're fifteen. We can go round and round the drive at Castlemore. You don't need a licence for that. It's private property.'

'You're nice to me,' Deirdre said frankly, and Fiona flushed with pleasure.

'I hope we'll always be friends,' she replied.

Two days later Norma, who was a cat lover, took Deirdre to one of the crofts on the estate belonging to Sandy MacPhail, and there she allowed Deirdre to choose two kittens from a recent litter. Deirdre's cup of happiness was full, almost to overflowing. Only occasionally did they come across her, silent and thoughtful, staring out of a window or sitting looking blindly across a room. When that happened they left her in peace.

At the end of October news reached Ardclune that Leona had had her second baby, another girl. She had been born in Rawalpindi and was to be called Mary. This time there was no question about it – there were to be no more children. Leona was quite ill.

Kenneth, who brought them the news, voiced his private feelings to Norma.

'What's to become of Ardclune?' he asked when they were alone. 'Finvola doesn't look like marrying. She's wedded to this ridiculous East End canteen for drunks she's become involved in. She's a religious crank and some grubby evangelical preacher has got her in his toils, and that's the fact of it. Leona won't have any sons now, which leaves only Torquil who is being brought up in Spain. Probably he won't want to live in Scotland.'

'Now how do you know that?' Norma answered comfortingly. 'You can't tell what the boy will want to do.'

'He's never been out of Spain. Dougal hasn't been home once, although Spain isn't all that far away.'

'It's a pity you can't visit him.'

'We should have taken the chance earlier. It's impossible now, with Andrew the way he is.'

'You could send Janet.'

'I know,' he smiled, 'but for some reason Janet doesn't want to go alone. I feel I've lost Dougal – and Torquil with him, although I've never laid eyes on the child. It's a ridiculous situation.'

'Anyway there's no saying whom Leona's two girls will marry. You're much too young to worry about what is going to happen to Ardclune.'

'Don't you ever worry about Castlemore?' Ken asked. He was exactly a year younger than Norma.

'Oh yes, sometimes, but I know it's pointless. I don't let it bother me too much. Besides, there's Pal Al now.'

'That's a ridiculous name for the poor boy.'

'I know, but it's stuck. Blame Fiona.'

'They could have called him Robert. It's one of his names.'

'It's their business, Ken.'

'I know. Don't mind me. I'm a bit out of sorts at this news that Leona can't have any more children. I was sure the next one would be a boy.'

'You're as bad as Angus MacLean at Mallaig, the one with the hotel.'

'Do I know him? What about him anyway?'

'He was mad to have a son, and they kept on trying. Everytime it was going to be a boy.'

'So what happened?' Ken asked suspiciously.

'He's got seven daughters and he's having a fine time trying to find husbands for them.'

'You're making that up.'

'You'll find five of them working in the Sleat Hotel if you go to Mallaig.'

'All right,' he laughed. 'I get the message. How's Alasdair in India?'

'I don't often get a letter from him, but from what Fiona tells me he seems to be enjoying life out there.'

'He would. I must be getting back. Deirdre looks so much better now.'

'She and Fiona are a tonic for one another. I'm very pleased with the way they have made friends.'

'It was a piece of luck Fiona coming home like that.'

'Yes.' Norma looked at him and smiled. 'I've often noticed that luck comes when you're least expecting it. Thank goodness it does.'

The end of the year saw more deaths, but not quite so close to home this time. Norma's parents, now Lord and Lady Beauly, had died together on the same day at their home, Beresford House, overlooking the Beauly Firth. They were very old and Norma had not seen them for several years, although generally they wrote once a year. The rift which had opened between them when they disowned Norma back in 1908 – at the time she discovered she was pregnant and had hurriedly married 'Dair' instead of his brother Donald – had never been healed. Guy and Edwina Beresford were stiff-necked and unbending people, and Norma had a pride of her own which made her keep her distance.

Her grief was superficial. Her father had been a vain

and ambitious man who was willing to sacrifice anything to political expediency. It had got him first a baronetcy and then a barony, and little good they did him as he had no sons, just Norma who cared nothing for his so-called honours.

She and Fiona took Deirdre over to Beresford House one week-end and they collected up various things they wanted to take back to Castlemore. The rest was left for sale. Norma was amused and not at all offended to learn that her father, who had ultimately made a great deal of money, had left her a thousand pounds and the contents of the house only. Everything else, which added up to over half a million pounds after payment of duty, went to the Episcopal Church in which he was a churchwarden. The great political party to which he belonged had confidently expected a large bequest and was disappointed. It was their own fault. Guy Beresford, not content with his titles, had demanded the Grand Cross of the Order of the Bath many years previously when he went out a lot and wanted a riband and a star to wear with evening dress. His demand was peremptory and accordingly had been turned down. He never forgot or forgave. The Church benefited by his meanness of spirit, but with half a million at stake who was going to trouble over anything so trivial as the matter of motive?

At the end of March 1937, Mary MacInnes came back to Castlemore for two weeks' holiday over Easter. With her she brought her fiancé, Flying Officer Robert Loring of the Royal Air Force. Loring was a fighter pilot who belonged to No. 1 Squadron at Tangmere. His home was Weobley, where Mary had her small cottage, and it was there that they had met during one of his leaves. They had become engaged six months previously, and this was the first the family had seen of him.

They arrived noisily in a bright red second-hand M.G. Sports, their luggage piled up in the back seat. Loring was tall and slim, with long fair hair and a ready smile.

He had charming manners and took nothing seriously. At first Norma didn't know what to make of him, he was so unlike the MacInnes men. He had far too much charm for her liking. Mary, however, was radiant and it was obvious that she was madly in love.

Norma followed her up to her room where she was unpacking, and sat on the bed and admired her daughter. Mary was smart and sophisticated – not at all the rather serious girl whose ambition had been to become a head librarian. She was still mad about books – half her luggage seemed to consist of novels – but her talk was of Loring. She called him Boy, which was his squadron nickname apparently. His father was a country doctor who lived in a charming old black and white house in the village of Weobley, and his mother was a parson's daughter. Robert Loring had been born in Nairobi in Kenya where his father had been a Government doctor for a few years. He had been in the R.A.F. since leaving school and had been commissioned in 1932.

'When's the wedding to be?' Norma asked.

'The end of June. We're getting married in Chichester. The squadron are giving us a party, you see, and we've got a little flat there, not too far from Tangers.'

'Where?'

'Tangers – Tangmere.'

'You've been there then?'

'Of course. We had a marvellous party when we were engaged.'

'I see.'

'Will you be able to come?'

'I don't know. It's a long journey, and it sounds like a wild party to me.'

'Well of course we'll have a party, Mummy.'

'I shan't know anyone. Would you be disappointed if I didn't come?'

'No,' Mary admitted honestly. 'Not very. As you say, it's a long way to travel just to see us married. We're going over to Deauville for a week's honeymoon.'

'Only a week?'

'Boy's in the aerobatic team, so we have to get back. He'll be at Hendon this year and they're competing at Zürich.'

'What exactly do they do?' Norma asked. She knew next to nothing about flying and the Royal Air Force.

Mary wondered how to describe an aerobatics display to her mother.

'They fly together,' she said rather lamely. 'Close to-gether – looping the loop and things like that. It's jolly clever.'

'It sounds dangerous.'

'It is, but they know what they're doing.'

'They have special aeroplanes, I suppose?'

'Yes, the squadron's got Hawker Furies. They're lovely.'

'You seem to know a lot about it.'

'Well, I've known Boy for two years,' Mary said defensively.

'Have you, May? You didn't tell me that.'

'It wasn't worth mentioning at first. I didn't know I was going to get engaged, did I?'

Norma smiled at her daughter's reaction.

'No of course not. You mustn't think I'm prying, darling. You forget how little I know. I'm interested, that's all.'

'Sorry, Mummy. I don't want you to disapprove. He's so splendid.'

'I can see you're in love anyway. I'm glad, but I shan't come to the wedding. You'll enjoy it more if there are no old sticks like me to spoil the fun. Are his parents going?'

'I don't think so. We'd rather hoped to have . . . well, to be with the boys.'

'I see.' Norma didn't really see at all. It was quite foreign to her own experience but she knew that this was part of the price of growing old. Mary was young and excited, and she wanted the company of other people of her own age.

'How old is Boy?' she asked.

'I told you, he's nearly twenty-four.'

'Did you? I'd forgotten. Is this his career, Mary?'

'Yes of course.'

'Then I suppose it's rather like being married to an Army officer.'

May did not contradict her mother although anyone with any sense knew that there was a world of difference between the fighter boys and stuffy old Army types. When she'd first told Boy that her brother was in the Army he'd laughed and said, 'Never mind, darling, I forgive you.' How could she possibly put any of this into words for Norma, who would never understand the difference between flying and doing guard duty or whatever it was they did in the Army?

They stayed for a week, and Wee Ken found Loring interesting to talk to. For his part Loring treated Ken with more respect than he generally showed towards his elders. After all, Ken had been an Observer in the R.F.C and deserved some respect. He did not get on nearly so well with Fiona. He'd put his foot in it from the start.

'I hear your husband is a brown job,' he said with a grin.

'I beg your pardon?' Fiona wondered what he was talking about.

'A brown job – Army.'

'Oh, yes. My husband is in the Army.' Fiona's voice became chilly. Her own family had no particular Army traditions, but she was Scots and proud of the Highland regiments in general and the Royal Grampian Highlanders in particular. There had been a few R.A.F. people on the Frontier of India, but no one took them at all seriously, and their officers did not have a very good reputation in Army circles.

38

'I suppose it's all right if you like that sort of thing, but I'd rather fly,' Loring said casually. It never crossed his mind that he was being rude. His set talked like this all the time.

'What sort of thing?' Fiona was not the very personification of icy politeness.

'Drill and guard duty and that sort of rot. Must be boring in peace time.'

'You should try a little duty on the North West Frontier, Mr Loring,' Fiona retorted frigidly, ignoring May who had appeared beside them anxiously, sensing something wrong. 'One of my husband's friends was captured by tribesmen. They recovered his body eventually. It was most unpleasant. The women torture the prisoners, you know, before killing them. But there, you wouldn't know about that sort of thing in the Air Force, I'm sure.'

Her tone was cutting and he flushed.

'I'm sorry,' he stammered, aghast at his own carelessness.

'I should hope you are.'

Fiona walked off and left them while he tried to explain lamely to the indignant May just how he had upset her sister-in-law. May saw only his side, of course, and never really liked Fiona after that.

Fiona wondered at herself. She at least knew something about flying and the gay and rather irresponsible young men who revelled in it. Never before had she been so hot under the collar on account of the wretched Army which had dragged her out to India a few weeks after her marriage, and which was therefore indirectly responsible for her illness and her present separation. She'd always thought Alasdair Beg's love for the regiment completely childish, yet she had quarrelled with Mary's fiancé on account of it. Eventually her sense of humour prevailed and she dismissed the incident from her mind.

They were married at the end of June and the family

sent off their presents and received boxes containing bits of wedding cake and an album of photographs, judging from the which the wedding was a very jolly affair indeed. It appeared that nobody over twenty-five had been present except Boy's commanding officer, who was not very much older anyway.

In late July Fiona took Pal Al to Castle Fearn for ten days. Her mother was far from well, and her younger brother was away in Edinburgh staying with friends. He would soon be in his last year at school and planned to go to university to get a law degree. It was nice to see home again, but she realized that it was no longer her home, that she had effectively left it behind her. Castlemore was where she belonged. After that visit she never felt homesick again.

She arrived back in time to help Norma kit out Deirdre for Miss Weir's Academy. They had to order much of the uniform in Perth itself from the official school outfitters, and the rest they were able to buy in Inverness. This kept them busy and happy for the remainder of the summer. Early in September they drove Deirdre to Perth where they spent the night at a hotel. Next day they delivered her over to her house mistress. Norma was well known at the school because of Mary and Elizabeth, as well as Finvola and Leona, her nieces. Fiona found it a wrench saying goodbye to Deirdre, even if it was only for three months until the Christmas holidays. When they returned to Castlemore it seemed dull and empty. Her feeling of loneliness soon vanished when a cable arrived one morning from India. It was from Alasdair Beg saying that he was sailing immediately for England. This was followed by a letter of explanation. He was going on a course at Salisbury after which he was being transferred to the 2nd battalion which was at the regimental depot at MacDonnel Barracks, Fort Augustus, a mere fifty miles from home.

Norma was as thrilled as Fiona.

40

'What luck his being transferred to the 2nd,' she exulted. 'Who'd have believed it?'

'Not Alasdair,' Fiona answered. 'He won't regard it as luck at all.'

'Oh nonsense, he'll be delighted to be with you and to see Pal Al.'

'Yes, he'll be glad to see us,' Fiona agreed, 'but he'll be furious at leaving the 1st. You'll see.'

'He'll get over that. He always liked the depot.'

Fiona said nothing, but she knew how very much more he liked active service. Now that the moment of his arrival was imminent, and unexpectedly so, she felt curiously unelated. She had a strange sensation that everything was happening to someone else and that she was merely an onlooker. A telegram from Tilbury preceded Alasdair's arrival in October. He came straight to Castlemore on a month's leave before going south to join his course.

The sight of his tanned, lean face, with its quiet air of confidence, did much to restore Fiona's spirits. She flew into his arms and they kissed passionately.

'Miss me, darling?' he asked, holding her at arm's length and inspecting her.

'Of course. It was awful.'

'You look well, more beautiful than ever. Having children is obviously good for you. Where is the young man?'

'In the morning room with Nanny. He plays there during the day. It saves going up and down stairs.'

Alasdair fussed over his son with unconcealed delight. Pal Al at two was sturdy and chubby. He regarded the stranger with suspicion, but after a little he thawed towards his father. Fiona fretted at having to share Alasdair with Norma that evening, and was not happy till they were together in the privacy of their bedroom. There she rested her head on his chest.

'Darling, will you be away for Christmas?' she asked.

'The course lasts till some time in February but I daresay we'll get leave. I'll drive up. I'm buying a new car, a Lagonda. It's a lovely piece of craftsmanship. I've ordered it and it should be ready when I get down to Salisbury.'

'So you'll be here till the middle of November, and you'll come back to the depot some time in February, is that right?'

'That's it.'

He was undressing and had just pulled off his shirt and vest.

'What's that?' she demanded suddenly. He turned to face her.

'Damn,' he answered without heat. 'I didn't mean you to see it.'

'How could I help but see it?' she demanded. 'You weren't thinking of separate bedrooms already, were you? Seriously, Alasdair, what happened?'

He glanced at the angry mark on his shoulder.

'An Afridi did it with one of those nasty long knives they like so much. It looks worse than it really is. It's that hideous purple mark.'

The scar was still livid.

'When did this happen?'

'About five months ago. I didn't mention it because I didn't want you worrying needlessly.'

She was stroking his shoulder gently and examining the wound.

'It went right through.'

'Yes, lucky it didn't do any real damage. It could have severed the muscle and then where would I have been?'

'What happened to the Afridi?' she asked curiously.

'I shot him.'

Fiona shivered as she listened.

'Sometimes I wish you weren't in the Army,' she said dully.

42

'What would I do then?' he grinned. 'A fine thing if I had no career, no job.'

'May's married to an R.A.F. officer.'

'She's got no sense of dignity,' Alasdair chuckled. 'My father will be revolving in his grave at the mere idea of it.'

'Let's go to bed,' she suggested.

'That's more like it. It's been a long time.'

That month was one of the happiest they had spent together. Most of the time Alasdair forgot completely about the Army. Only once did he insist on taking them both into Fort William to visit Captain Wallace. Wallace, who was nearly sixty-five now, had been Regimental Sergeant Major of MacDonnel's Loyal Regiment in which Alasdair's father had been commissioned. Wallace had been commissioned in the field, and had won the Distinguished Service Order and the Military Cross as well as the Distinguished Conduct Medal with Bar. Alasdair Beg had known him since childhood, and still remembered vividly the day when Wallace had come to Castlemore carrying his father's sword and pistol. He had been with the Colonel on his last night before the attack in which he perished and was awarded a posthumous D.S.O. It was William Wallace who had taught him his foot drill and sword drill when he was still a schoolboy, so that he had gone to Sandhurst with more idea of what it was all about than the average gentleman cadet.

'So, this is your son!' Wallace exclaimed, bending over the baby. 'He'll be going into the regiment, of course.'

'Of course,' Alasdair Beg agreed without a moment's hesitation, and for a second Fiona felt angry.

Would the child be allowed to decide nothing for himself?

While Alasdair brought Captain Wallace up to date on the regiment's doings in India, Fiona and Mrs Wallace went into the kitchen and made tea and talked about less warlike things. They stayed quite late, for Alasdair was reluctant to leave once the whisky bottle was out and they

43

had settled down to a good old Army gossip. When they did go finally Fiona was nettled.

'You might have some consideration for the baby,' she reprimanded him. 'We should have been home an hour ago. It's after his bath time.'

'Let him miss his bath then. He's clean enough.'

The subject of this discussion was curled up on the back seat of the car, blissfully asleep.

'You are thoughtless,' she could not resist telling him.

'I wanted Willie Wallace to see him. You don't know how much it means to Willie. He worshipped the ground my father walked on, and he was like a second father to me in some ways. I wish we had another Wallace in the regiment nowadays. The two battalions put together wouldn't make one of him.'

'Oh you and your battalions,' she snapped.

'What's the matter with you?' Alasdair asked, surprised.

'I'm tired of the Army.'

'It's a bit late for that, darling, isn't it?' he drawled, very cool. 'You should have thought of that before you married me. I never pretended to be anything but a soldier, did I?'

'No,' she admitted grudgingly, 'but I had no idea it was an obsession.'

'Obsession? You're overstating it.'

'No I'm not. It's all you think about, the wretched regiment. I don't know why you wanted a wife at all.'

'I happened to love you. I still do. That's the only reason I married you. I wasn't recruiting wives for the Army, you know.'

She laughed as she did so often at the end of their little quarrels. He had the knack of saying the right thing to change her mood.

'All right, but I hope you'll give Pal Al a chance to make up his own mind over what he wants to do when he grows up.'

'Of course I will. I shan't mind if he chooses the Gordon Highlanders instead – so long as he has a damned good reason.'

'Oh you, you're incorrigible,' she retorted, but she leaned her head on his shoulder as she said it.

3

Having Alasdair Beg at home made a tremendous difference to Castlemore. A house minus its master is not the same place at all. Norma in particular felt the difference. Her husband and her father-in-law had both died in 1917. Her mother-in-law had died in 1922, the year in which Alasdair Beg had gone off as a boarder to Lamond's School in Pitlochry. She had been the solitary chatelaine of Castlemore for too many years and she enjoyed it when Alasdair was at home. The effect was noticed, too, by the four men on the staff – Mr Love the portly and somewhat pompous butler, Fraser the footman, Inglis the chauffeur-handyman, and MacOmie the gardener. Norma managed the staff very well, all eight of them, but she never felt quite so confident dealing with men as she did with her own sex.

One of Alasdair's first acts was to visit Ardclune to talk business with Wee Ken. Wee Ken had inherited Merchant Bob's ability with money and was financial adviser to both Norma and Alasdair. Only Charles had scorned Wee Ken's advice and gone his own way, with the result that Charles's handsome patrimony had almost disappeared and he had to count the cost of every box of cigars. Tradesmen were often forced to wait for their accounts to be paid.

Despite high taxation and crippling death duties, Alasdair and Norma were financially very sound. Norma had about two hundred and fifty thousand pounds invested, and Alasdair Beg well over a hundred thousand. Mary and Betty had had no capital of their own, but Norma gave Mary an allowance of £750 a year and Betty, who had lived free at Castlemore, had had a smaller one of £400 until her death. Unemployment and depression were meaningless words in the family.

Wee Ken poured a whisky for his nephew and himself and settled down in his favourite leather armchair in the study.

'*Slainthe*,' he toasted, raising his glass. 'You look fit, young fellow.'

'I am,' Alasdair laughed. 'I ought to be. I've had a wonderful two and a half years on the Frontier.'

'Sorry to have left it?'

'Truthfully? Yes, I am, but don't you dare to say so to Fiona. She wouldn't understand, but what wouldn't I give for a whiff of early morning air up in the passes? The North West Frontier is soldiering at its best. It's far more interesting than home service, and at the same time it isn't brutal and soul destroying like trench warfare must have been. It's no use trying to explain. Kipling knew what it was like. Read him.'

'I have,' Wee Ken grinned. 'Enjoy yourself while you can. The way things are going in Europe we aren't so far removed from another war. You can see it coming.'

'Do you think so?' Alasdair asked, leaning forwards.

'I'm no prophet. Maybe it will all blow over, but Hitler is playing a dangerous game. All the talk is of appeasement but you can't appease a wolf, can you? You can't make friends with a mad dog.'

'They say he's done a lot for Germany.'

'Of course he has. That's only one side of the picture.

I say we'll be lucky to escape another major European war. The trouble is that no one knows what the next one will be like. If Spain is anything to go by, it will be quite as nasty as the last one, even if in a different way.'

'I hope you're wrong. I don't mind going away and fighting if I have to, but I don't want the Germans dropping bombs on my wife and children.'

'Don't think they won't,' Kenneth said with a shrug.

'You're a gloomy one today, aren't you? I came to talk about money.'

'I'm better qualified to discuss that,' Ken laughed.

'I'm interested in this new South American development scheme.'

'The Ranitser Corporation?'

'Yes. They're paying handsome dividends.'

'I don't think it's proved itself yet,' Ken said cautiously. 'I'd leave it for a year or two.'

'Yes, and watch the price of shares rocket upwards. A new issue has just been announced. I'd like to apply for some.'

'Suit yourself. Your money is all in the motor-car industry, in clothing and in food. If there's a war, all three are as safe as houses. People will buy all the food and clothing they can get their hands on, and the Forces will be using vehicles at a tremendous rate. Of course, I move the money around from company to company depending on how they're doing, but basically these are the three things I invest in. It was your father's principle and I've always found it sound. It may not be as startling as South African mining or industrials, but it pays handsomely.'

'There's a chance of a killing in Ranitser. I know a chap whose father is a stockbroker and he tipped me off. Ranitser are on to something. Look at their last dividend.'

'The question is, can they keep it up? What's got into you, Alasdair? You never used to worry about big killings on the stock market. That's not how the family has

47

prospered. Our money is well spread in things we understand and can keep an eye on. About a third of our money,
yours, mine and Norma's, is in American cars. The rest is
in British companies. I did think of having a little fling
in the aircraft industry, but I'm not entirely sure. If you
want to try something new, why not put a little into
Douglas and Boeing in the U.S.A. and see what happens
to it?'

'No, I'm not interested in that. If my information is
right, I can double my money in a year.'

Ken poured two more whiskies and thought carefully
as he did so. Alasdair Beg was twenty-seven, he was
not a child. It would be a pity to upset him by too much
plain speaking. It might only drive him further along the
road, and it was a road Wee Ken did not trust.

'Listen,' he said, keeping his relaxed air, 'I've learned
one thing. There's no safe way of doubling your money
in a year. People do manage it and I've read of people
trebling their capital in three months – so have you, in
all probability. It can be done, but only by taking the most
enormous risks. A great many people have been wiped
out by being in too much of a hurry to make a profit. In
the long term there is no such thing as quick money. I've
watched the market for years. I'm not a stockbroker, of
course and I've only been interested in one thing – a safe
investment with a good return, never an unsafe investment with a better return.'

'I know all this,' Alasdair said impatiently. 'I wasn't
proposing to put everything into Ranitser.'

That's a relief, Wee Ken thought.

'How much then?' he asked, almost idly.

'Two-thirds, just for a year. At the end of the year I'll
take my profit and get out.'

That's what you say, Ken thought. He knew better. If
there was a big yield in a year, Alasdair would be unable
to resist the temptation to leave it in for another year, and
another, until in the fourth or fifth, if it lasted so long,

it all went crash and the paper millionaire was wiped out. That was the classic pattern.

'That's a lot,' he mused, his expression showing nothing of his alarm.

'It leaves me about thirty-five thousand soundly invested, doesn't it? Ranitser won't go bust in a year. In fact they'll probably never go bust. I've got good information.'

'How good?'

'I told you, this chap's father is a stockbroker.'

'Who is this chap?'

'I met him on the boat coming home. He's Indian cavalry – Prince Albert Victor's Own – and he was coming back for a spot of leave. He knows a lot about it, because of his father, you see.'

'Uh-huh.' Ken's face was expressionless. If Alasdair was anything like his father – and he was like his father in almost everything – he would know almost nothing at all about the handling of money. But whereas Dair had had the good sense to realize his shortcomings and accept advice, young Alasdair had been listening to glowing stories from a brother officer, and his head had been turned.

'Tell me,' Ken said, desperately thinking of some way to head off his nephew. 'Why the hurry? You've been away on the Frontier for a long time. Why not watch developments in *The Times* for a few months before making up your mind about anything?'

'There isn't time,' Alasdair assured him confidently. 'I must act quickly if I'm to get in on the ground floor with Ranitser. Now will you do it for me, or shall I get myself a stockbroker? Which would you prefer?'

'I think,' Ken said slowly, 'it would be better if you acted through a stockbroker. After all, I'm simply an amateur.'

'You're not offended?'

'Of course not, but I do think you're being hasty.'

'Well if I make fifty or a hundred thousand in twelve months, don't say I didn't tip you off.'

'I shan't,' Ken promised drily.

It could have been worse. If Alasdair realized two-thirds of his current shareholdings now, he might get as much as £80,000. It left almost £40,000, which was not to be sneezed at. The money was bringing in a very sound overall nine per cent, so that even after taxation £40,000 would give Alasdair a substantial income. What worried Ken was that the family had not produced a single money earner for a century. General Charles had added nothing to his wealth, on the contrary he had lived on his substantial income. Admittedly Merchant Bob had increased his capital handsomely, but only by investment and he had never run a business or controlled an industry. They were all the same. They lived on the proceeds of a West Indian fortune made a very long time ago. They'd lived in moderate luxury and they'd actually increased their capital quite a lot. Merchant Bob, after all, had had five sons to provide for, and he had done so in no uncertain fashion. It was solid achievement. Against that, if they were wiped out financially, not one of them would know how to earn money.

It would be a sad day for Alasdair if he had to live on his Army pay. He, Kenneth, made a little out of his land, but not enough to support Ardclune House and an idiot son who needed a full-time nurse. Their survival depended largely on their ability to maintain their wealth, to guard it, to protect it. This was why he was so apprehensive of putting money into a wild-cat scheme which promised huge gains on the short term. If one had to put money in South America, and for the life of him he could see no justification for anything so rash, then there were the railways and Argentine beef. Ranitser was a flash in the pan and Ken had an instinctive distrust of mining. Ranitser had made some important discoveries of mineral deposits, but they had as yet produced nothing substantial. The whole thing was far too risky, and he knew that Merchant Bob would never have approved.

Alasdair cared nothing for his uncle's fears. He put two-thirds of his money into the wonder company and then, two weeks later, decided to put in another twenty thousand pounds. Ken knew nothing of this. He had no longer any direct dealings with Alasdair's money.

Christmas of 1937 was a happy one, with Alasdair back home. On Boxing Day they all visited Ardclune and had a family party there. Deirdre was suddenly growing up into a very mature young woman. She seemed far older than her thirteen years. It was obvious she was going to have considerable charm when she grew up. Norma felt a particular affection for Bobbie's daughter, the more so now that she herself had been relieved of the burden of Betty's suffering. Betty's death had been a happy release for Norma as well as for Betty. With May away in Sussex with her husband, Fiona and Deirdre now took the place of her own daughters. Watching Deirdre's steady progress, and seeing Fiona and Alasdair together, filled her with enormous happiness. Norma had always found her happiness in other people.

Alasdair went back to Salisbury after the Christmas break, and did not return till the end of February. When he did, he was exultant. His promotion to Captain had finally come through and he was going to the 2nd battalion as acting Adjutant. Strangely enough this first taste of desk duty did not irk him at all. The reason was not difficult to find. Alasdair loved the regiment, and the insight he got as Adjutant into the inner workings of the 2nd battalion fascinated him. Like his father, he made a fetish of efficiency. The work was all that mattered. Just as he had been an outstanding company officer so he made an outstanding Adjutant. Nothing was too much trouble for him. He and his new Commanding Officer, Lieutenant-Colonel Gordon MacRae, D.S.O., O.B.E., rapidly became friends.

Alasdair and Fiona discussed the idea of trying to rent a house near to the barracks at Fort Augustus, at the lower end of Loch Ness. In the end the subject was dropped. Norma, who had gone through the same performance with Dair, was amused to watch the process repeated. There was one important difference, however, of which she was not aware. When she had married Dair in 1908 it had been Dair who did not want the distraction of a wife just outside barracks. With Fiona it was different. Alasdair certainly preferred to divide his life into two compartments – the week-days spent at Fort Augustus and the week-ends spent at Castlemore. Yet even if this had not been so, Fiona would have been reluctant to exchange the comforts of Castlemore for lodgings. A rented house, however excellent, was not home.

The signs of war were becoming plainer. On the 14th of February 1938 the Singapore Naval Base was opened – an odd sort of proceeding for St Valentine's Day as Wee Ken remarked sarcastically to Janet. A month later, on the 13th of March, Germany finally annexed Austria. The signs were now clear, but timid men afraid of war were equally afraid to read them and Europe remained splendidly, one might almost say devotedly, unprepared.

Then they heard from Paris, via Rome. Charles had died on the 17th of April. His wife Vivienne wrote curtly to Gordon in Richmond, Virginia, and to Susan in Rome. Susan at once wrote to Wee Ken and Norma. It was several weeks before the contents of Charles's will became known to them. His money, and very little of it there had been at the end, he had left to his stony-hearted French wife. Grunaglack House, however, with all its expensive contents bought by June Haverford after their marriage in 1910, was left to both Gordon and Susan.

Gordon, pursuing his own gilt-edged career in the Fairfax Corporation, was not in the least interested in the old house standing between Fort William and Lochy Bridge. He offered to sell his interest in it to Susan for three thousand pounds and she accepted promptly. Lord Maurice wrote out the necessary cheque, which left a sizable hole in his small capital. It was obvious that Gordon MacInnes had no intention of returning to Scotland. Several months previously, in June of 1937, Annabelle had presented him with a son, called Charles after his grandfather. The giant Fairfax Corporation was still controlled by the Fairfax family, and Annabelle and the new baby Charles were in the direct line of succession.

Finally, at the beginning of June, Norma received a letter from Susan in Rome saying that she and the children were returning to Scotland to live at Grunaglack, and asking Norma if she could help over the matter of servants. The letter raised one or two tricky points, for Susan had written airily to say that she would like 'whatever servants you think fit, whatever you have yourself'. Norma, wealthy in her own right, had a total of eight servants. Would Susan want so many? The answer appeared to be yes, especially as Grunaglack was a larger house and considerably older, although as a property it wasn't a patch on the family showpiece, Castlemore. The question was, what could Susan afford? Norma knew very little about the Blood finances. Susan had no money of her own, and Lord Maurice was a younger son. Was his father, the Marquess of Minchinhampton, wealthy – and if wealthy, had he provided for his younger sons or not? Some people didn't. Younger sons did not count for very much.

Norma earmarked a cook, a housemaid and a gardener and had them standing by. Susan could make her own arrangements.

Fiona had been living in a quietly delightful world of her own since March, when it was clearly established that she was having another child. This time she was certain it would be the girl she had wanted so much before. It was not that she did not love her first-born. She was a conscientious mother and lavished affection on Pal Al, but behind it all was the certain knowledge that he would be torn from her. At the age of twelve he would be sent to Lamond's in Pitlochry. There had been some talk of sending him to an English public school, and Alasdair had toyed with the idea of putting his name down for Harrow, but it had come to nothing. It would be Lamond's, because that's where the MacInneses went. After that it would be the Royal Grampians because that, too, was where MacInneses went. A tradition had been founded, and Fiona knew her husband too well to imagine that he would deviate from it by a hairsbreadth.

She longed for a daughter, for a child who would grow up to to be her friend, a child whose life she could share. The truth was that she simply could not share her husband's veneration for the Highland Brigade, and above all for the Grampians. She concealed her heresy from him, and also from Norma. She did not know exactly what Norma felt about it all but she realized that Norma accepted the situation. Fiona did not accept it. In her heart she was a rebel.

Alasdair was sublimely unaware of his wife's inner feelings. He shared her delight about the baby and assumed that she, like himself, would want another son. It was the obvious thing to do.

Susan Blood arrived late in June 1938 with her two sons, Vernon aged four and Philip aged two. They were fair-haired like their mother, rather attractive boys, very clean and neat, with manners so perfect that Norma thought them unnatural. Norma had arranged everything in advance. The house had been opened up, aired, cleaned, bedrooms had been got ready, the drive had been tidied up and there was plenty of food to see them through the first week. It had taken quite a lot of Norma's time, which she did not grudge one little bit, for she enjoyed doing things for other people. Fiona had helped. There were flowers in all the rooms, and the silverware and brassware gleamed.

Norma lent Susan her own lady's maid, Jean, for two days to help her settle in. They left Jean to unpack everything, and came straight over to Castlemore for lunch with the family. Seven years of marriage had left no marks on Susan. She did not look a day older than she had done on her wedding day. Her patrician attitudes, however, had thrived on Embassy life, and Norma was greatly amused by it all. She lived up to her husband's courtesy title.

'How is Maurice?' Norma asked as they drank sherry before lunch.

'Very well, thank you. He couldn't get away, unfortunately, but will come home later in the year for a short visit.'

'You'll be staying at Grunaglack alone?'

'Yes.' Susan stared at her aunt. 'I'm tired of foreigners. We've never had a house of our own, you see. I shall have to spend a fortune on it.'

'Will you?' Norma asked, taken aback.

'Of course. I shall want central heating, and all that furniture is ghastly. It's only fit for burning.'

'Oh.' Norma and Fiona exchanged silent glances.

'Do I understand that there are only three servants?'

'I wasn't sure what you'd need, so I engaged a cook, a housemaid and a gardener. I thought that would do you for a few weeks until you've settled down.'

'I shall certainly need a lady's maid. Thank you for lending me yours.'

'Not at all.'

'We had ten servants in Rome,' Susan said rather disdainfully.

'Really?' Norma could not think what they wanted with ten servants.

'Yes, we entertained almost every evening.'

55

'I expect you'll be able to entertain at Grunaglack once you make friends.'

Obviously Lord Maurice was not completely short of money.

'Do you entertain much?'

'Never.'

'Never? What on earth do you do?'

'We live here,' Norma said simply, and Fiona gave her full marks. She did not like Lady Maurice Blood at all. She was much too overpowering. It was difficult to remember that she was less than two years older than Fiona herself.

The children sat silently, and Fiona tried to strike up a conversation with them after lunch, but they were either shy or suspicious. They had nothing to say for themselves.

The following evening Janet gave a dinner for them all at Ardclune, and Norma and Fiona went, leaving Pal Al at home with the Nanny. The first thing that happened was that Susan telephoned rather testily to ask Ken where the car was. 'The car?'

'Aren't you sending a car for me?'

'I'm sorry, I thought you had one.'

'Not yet. I haven't had time to buy a car and engage a chauffeur.'

'I'm very sorry. I'll come round straight away.'

'There's no need to come yourself, send the chauffeur.'

'I don't have one,' Ken retorted.

There was a silence, and then, 'Oh, I see. I thought everyone had a chauffeur.'

Ken managed to hang up before letting out a howl of laughter. It was several seconds before he was able to tell the others what had taken place.

'What's got into her?' he spluttered. 'She was quite a nice child.'

'She's Lady Maurice of the Embassy,' Janet told him bluntly.

'Oh pooh. Blood isn't an Ambassador. He's a First Secretary or something quite junior.'

'Janet's right,' Norma smiled. 'I'm afraid Susan has turned out to be a snob.'

'Well,' Ken said weakly, 'I offered to go and drive her over. I'd better be on my way. Sorry, darling, it means dinner will be a little late.'

Ken got out his old Daimler and made the nine-mile journey to Grunaglack. Susan gave him a somewhat chilly reception and climbed into the back seat.

'How are the boys?' Ken asked as he drove off.

'In bed.'

'They're well?'

'Yes. Am I early?'

'Early? No, we were expecting you twenty minutes or more ago. I'm sorry I didn't think about transport. Very stupid of me.'

'Don't you dress for dinner?'

Kenneth stared at the road ahead. He was wearing an expensive, dark lounge suit. He *had* dressed for dinner. Frequently he just wore the kilt or tweed suit he'd been wearing all day.

'I didn't realize you were so informal in the country,' Susan went on.

Ken still did not reply. She was Charles's daughter and Charles was the sort of pretentious ass who would wear a dinner jacket even if the heavens fell. He felt he had to make allowances for her.

'We don't usually bother,' he said mildly.

'One should. It is too easy to become lax.'

Ken could hardly wait to tell Janet. He did not have to. Susan did so on arrival, explaining volubly that she had no idea they were so careless of appearances in the country. She herself wore a simply gorgeous long dress and a diamond necklace and ear-rings. She was a beauty all right, but totally out of place, yet they had to admire the way she carried it off. She made *them* feel awkward. It was no mean achievement.

For the next week or two things were quiet and they did not see very much of Susan, although she telephoned frequently with various questions. After she had been back about six weeks Susan gave a small dinner party. Kenneth telephoned Norma.

'Norma, did you get an invitation to Susan's tonight?'
'Yes.'

'I suppose we'd better dog up, hadn't we? After what happened last time I'm not sure whether to wear a black tie or a white – assuming I can find either.'

'I think it will be a black-tie occasion,' Norma laughed.

'Oh lord, I hate it. It's only a meal.'

'You never know who else she has invited,' Norma pointed out.

'I thought it would be just family.'

'Did she say so?'

'No,' Ken admitted. 'I see what you mean. Long dresses and black ties it is then.'

When Norma and Fiona arrived they were admitted by a footman and shown into the big drawing room where another footman was offering drinks on a tray. There were five people. Susan introduced them. Norma had neither seen nor heard of them before, but that was not very surprising because, as she had told Susan, she did not entertain. There were two retired couples from near Ballachulish with the sort of over-refined accents which immediately made Norma suspicious, and a young man who was introduced as a Major on leave and whose father seemingly owned a factory and was a County Councillor. Norma wondered how Susan had contrived to meet them all in such a short time.

She and Fiona kept together, feeling distinctly out of it. The talk was of county families, many of whom Norma knew by reputation, a few of whom she had met. There was much use of Christian names, rather loud laughter.

Ken, when he arrived, was taken aback, but Janet had met the young Major somewhere and was promptly involved in a long conversation about her own three brothers in the Scots Greys.

The dinner was elaborate and the service was poor. Susan glared at the two footmen, which did not help matters at all. She also stared frostily at her relatives who were contributing nothing to the festiveness of the occasion. Altogether it was an awkward meal and when the ladies withdrew after dinner, leaving the four men to the brandy, Susan turned to Norma.

'Are you not feeling well, Aunt Norma?'

'I feel very well, thank you.'

'I wondered. You were so quiet.'

'I couldn't think of anything to say,' Norma explained calmly, leaving Susan speechless.

At long last the agony was over and they left. Kenneth left Janet sitting in the front of the Daimler and strolled over to the Rolls.

'I hope that doesn't happen again for a long time,' he told Norma. 'What a ghastly performance.'

'She hasn't been home long,' Norma pointed out, making allowances.

'The two footmen are hired from Fort William. I found that out. The cooking, however, was plain bad. What's the use of putting on a splash if you haven't got a decent cook?'

'How do you know about the footmen?' Fiona asked, curious.

'I asked one of them how long he'd worked for Susan,' Ken grinned.

'Oh, Ken!'

'Well, why not? Bad food badly served – it wasn't worth getting dressed for. The people too, a rum lot. I shall acquire a headache if I'm asked again.'

'I don't think we're likely to be asked often,' Fiona said gently. 'I think Susan found us an embarrassment.'

'She was such a nice child,' Norma said with a sigh, and on that generous note they said good night.

They heard little from Grunaglack thereafter. On Sunday the 4th of September a baby girl was born at Castlemore. It was an easy birth and Alasdair, who was home for the week-end, was delighted by the timing. He had wanted to be present this time. If he was disappointed that it was a girl, he concealed the fact.

'What are we going to call her?' he asked Fiona. 'You've never told me what we'd do about a girl.'

'Frances Mary.'

'Really? Is that someone we know? Is the Mary for my sister?'

'Certainly not,' Fiona exclaimed. 'I got the name from a book. I think it's beautiful. She's to be called Frances Mary – not Frances, or Mary, but both.'

'Good lord. Well, it's your say-so. What book anyway?'

'A book by Maurice Walsh. You haven't read it.'

'You and your books. I don't know what you see in them.' Then he smiled quickly. 'Are you feeling all right, darling?'

'Perfectly all right, thank you.'

'Do you know, I was quite scared, waiting. I was so afraid something would happen to you.'

'There was nothing to worry about,' Fiona told him, glancing at him with interest. 'You weren't really scared, were you?'

'Cross my heart.' He leaned over and kissed her on the lips. 'I love you. Don't you realize that yet? The children don't really matter – you're the one who counts.' He put an arm round her and stroked her forehead gently. 'If anything happened to you I don't know what I'd do.'

'Go on, you've got the Army.'

He was silent. 'Yes,' he agreed at last, 'but it would never be the same. You can't just have one thing in your life.'

She gave him an amused smile. It was a funny way of putting it, but she knew what he meant.

'I'd never look at another woman,' he said quietly. 'You know that, don't you?'

'Darling,' she laughed, 'what's got into you? Do I look suspicious?'

'No, I just wanted you to know.'

'Alasdair my dear, you're the soul of honour. Of course I trust you.'

'Yes, but I wouldn't even *want* to look at another woman,' he insisted.

'You are flattering, all of a sudden. We must have babies more often.'

'I don't know that I could go through it again.'

'You're priceless,' she laughed. 'I tell you what. We'll change places. I'm sure I could go through it, if all I had to do was wait.'

'You're making a joke of it, but it was no joke.'

'I'm sorry,' she apologized contritely. 'Kiss me again.'

The crisis in Europe was reaching a peak. On the 28th of September the Royal Navy was mobilized and it seemed that the worst had happened. On the next day, however, the Munich agreement was signed, and a triumphant Neville Chamberlain returned to Britain, certain that war had been averted.

Many people believed him, because people wanted to believe him. There was rejoicing everywhere, but not by everyone. To others Chamberlain had brought not peace but a momentary respite, a postponement of the inevitable war. Nothing was going to stop Hitler's land grabbing.

Alasdair and Wee Ken were among the prophets of war. When Frances Mary was christened in Fort William on Sunday 2nd October, Alasdair found himself wondering what sort of world his children would grow up into. Standing in church that morning he had an uncharacteristic onset of doubts. His own father had been a regular Army officer, and he had lost his life in the last war. Was it to be his own fate to do the same? That was what the regular Army was for, to take the brunt of the assault while the country mobilized. Not many regular combatant soldiers survived wars. If war came he would probably end up either a General or a rotting corpse in some new No Man's Land.

For a fleeting second he felt the trailing fingers of panic. He did not want to be taken away from his wife and children, he did not want to go away and never see Castlemore again. He hadn't felt like this on the Frontier, why did he feel it now? he wondered. The moment passed and his confidence returned.

He was not afraid of the future.

4

In April of 1939 Leona and Sir Lauchlan, 'Rajah Sahib', came home from India on six months' leave. Janet and Kenneth were overjoyed to see their two grandchildren, for they had never seen young Torquil in Spain. Eve, the elder MacKinnon child, had had her fourth birthday on the P. & O. steamer on the way home and Mary was a little over two. They drove to Castlemore on their first Saturday at home, and Alasdair took Rajah Sahib off to the study and offered him a cigar and a glass of sherry. Sir Lauchlan was almost seven years Alasdair's senior, a tall, dark, hawk-nosed man in his thirty-sixth year. He wore an air of easy authority which impressed Alasdair, himself accustomed to authority.

'What do you think of the news?' Alasdair asked.

'Not much. War is inevitable.'

'That's what I think.'

'I'm glad they sent me home. I wouldn't like to be stuck in India while there was a war in Europe.'

'Aren't you going back?'

'No. At the end of my leave in September I'm going to the India Office in London.'

'Is that good? Promotion?'

'Yes, it is. In a way I'm sorry. If things had been different I'd have refused to go, but if there's going to be a war we want to be back in Britain.'

'Quite. How does it feel after all these years?'

'A little strange. The country seems so small. Still, we're all coming home. You're home, Susan's home, and now we're home. I believe Blood is returning this summer also.'

'Is he?'

'So Susan told us the other day. I don't mean he'll be in this country permanently, but his spell in Italy is finished. I imagine he'll get some leave and be sent off somewhere else. Funny business, Susan coming back alone.'

'I gathered she doesn't like foreigners nowadays.'

'It's her husband's job, isn't it?' Rajah Sahib asked bluntly.

'Yes,' Alasdair grinned. 'I don't think that cuts much ice with Susan. We don't see her often.'

Rajah Sahib grunted. 'I rather gathered from her tone that she didn't entirely approve of the rest of the family. There was something about Kenneth not dressing for dinner.'

'That's right. I heard about it from Fiona. It seems Susan thinks one should dress for dinner every night, come what may.'

'Some people do,' Rajah Sahib remarked. He himself mostly had to. 'I find it a pleasant change to live informally. There was far too much of the other thing in India.

63

I don't envy Blood,' he added quite casually.

Alasdair looked at his cousin's husband with fresh interest. He didn't really know MacKinnon well. There was something about him, though – it was almost like speaking to a brother Army officer.

'He may like her as she is,' Alasdair said in reply. 'Anyway it's none of my business. I don't pay much attention.'

'Quite right. I'd like to visit your barracks some time.'

'Would you really? I wonder if you'd care to dine with us?'

'Very much.'

'I'll put your name down then. Probably it will be next month. There's an At Home in June too. I hope you and Leona will both come. We do them rather well.'

'Fine. Incidentally I got to know some of your chaps last year, the 1st battalion. I was in Rawalpindi and so were they.'

They talked about regimental personalities for a time, and then went out for a stroll in the grounds. There were daffodils and late crocuses everywhere, and the pale spring sun glinted on the waters of the loch at the foot of the garden.

'You've got a fair bit of land here, haven't you?' Rajah Sahib asked.

'Yes. There are about twenty acres of grounds to the house and we have another four hundred acres up behind the trees there. It doesn't produce much of course. There are seven small crofts but the rents haven't gone up for years. When my great-great-grandfather bought this place it was the house he wanted, not the land.'

'It's very beautiful. I wish we had something like it.'

'Ardclune's nice.'

'Agreed, but it isn't ours you know. Leona has a brother and a sister, quite apart from Andrew.'

'Will Leona be going to London with you?'

'I don't know. Normally she would, but if war comes

she'd be better off in the country. Anyway there's no hurry to decide.'

'No, I suppose not. It must be nice to have six months' leave.'

'It is, rather. I've had no leave for six years. It works out at about a month a year.'

'When you put it like that it isn't so much,' Alasdair laughed.

About a month later Rajah Sahib went to Fort Augustus for the evening. He was to dine in mess with the 2nd Royal Grampians. It was a colourful occasion. The officers were splendid in their scarlet mess jackets with gold buttons, scarlet and buff facings. With them they wore Glengarry tartan kilts and long white sporrans mounted with gold, tartan hose and buckled patent leather brogues – an impressive sight. All the mess silver was on display, and as MacDonnel's had been one of the wealthier regiments once, this was equally grand.

Sir Lauchlan was very much an honoured guest because of his baronetcy. Somewhat to Alasdair's surprise, Rajah Sahib had blossomed forth in a kilt. It had never occurred to Alasdair that he possessed one. He wore a black velvet doublet with silver buttons, and under his white bow tie nestled the badge of a Companion of the Order of the Star of India. He was as distinguished as, if a little less gaudy than, his hosts.

He was monopolized by Colonel MacRae who had no intentions of leaving such a distinguished guest to the tender mercies of the junior officers.

'I've been meaning to ask my cousin something for a long time,' Rajah Sahib said during dinner. 'Perhaps you can satisfy my curiosity.'

'I'll try,' MacRae agreed.

'The regiment was originally called MacDonnel's, wasn't it? With two "n's" and one "l"?'

'Yes,' MacRae smiled. 'You want to know why, when we were raised by the younger brother of MacDonnell of

Glengarry who spells it differently?'

'Yes.'

'Simple. Something you'll probably appreciate being in the Indian Civil Service. When the name was originally published in the Army list it was mis-spelled and it stayed that way for about five years before someone spotted it. It was too late by then. Why nobody noticed it I can't say except that often it's difficult to notice a mis-spelling in a very familiar name. Glengarry raised absolute hell trying to get it changed, but the Secretary of War was adamant. He wasn't going to alter the name after five years. It was quite a hot engagement I believe.' He smiled at Lauchlan. 'Now of course we're proud of the spelling mistake. It adds a little touch of distinction. Unfortunately as we're now the Royal Grampians, we don't use the name MacDonnel very often.'

Although he had never had the slightest military inclinations himself, and had always felt that the Army in India should be under the complete control of the Indian Civil Service, Lauchlan could see what the attraction was to someone like Alasdair, with his schoolboy code of honour and his love of pageantry and tradition. He also saw, and was heartened by the fact, that the officers of the Grampians had a very professional outlook. There was considerable talk of war, but there was no puerile jingoism in the Grampians' attitude. They took the prospect of war very seriously and knew it would be a desperate struggle. They seemed to have a healthy respect for the Germans.

In June he and Leona went to the At Home with Alasdair, Fiona and Norma. There was a green lawn with gay flower beds near the barracks square, overlooked by the Sergeants' Mess and the Officers' Mess. Here a marquee had been erected. Pipers played outside, 'at a safe distance', as Leona whispered to Sir Lauchlan, and white-gloved and white-jacketed mess waiters carried round trays of champagne and whisky. Everyone was in civilian clothes and almost all the men wore a kilt. Captain Wallace had come up from Fort Willian and he and Norma had a long talk together. Colonel MacRae also monopolized Norma to a considerable extent. Dair was regarded as the most illustrious of the regiment's commanding officers, and it was under his command that the 1st Battalion had been nicknamed The Devil's Own. His widow held a very special place in their hearts.

In July, May came home on a short visit with Boy Loring. He had been promoted to Flight Lieutenant and earlier in the year he had been awarded the Air Force Cross. Fiona still regarded him with suspicion and there was a distinct coolness between May and herself, but Loring and Alasdair quickly became friends.

When they had gone back to the south of England, Fiona told Alasdair about her little scene with Loring. To her relief Alasdair laughed.

'Serve him right,' he said. 'He's not a bad sort, though.'

'I noticed you were fairly friendly.'

'Yes, I like him. Don't let that rather effete, bored manner of his put you off. You don't get the A.F.C. for nothing, and he's a member of that aerobatic team – he's got plenty of guts.'

'I'm afraid your sister will never forgive me.'

'You don't want to bother about May,' Alasdair laughed. 'She was always a strange creature. She'll get over it.'

At last the uneasy peace broke. In September Britain was once again at war with Germany. The 2nd Batalion was ordered south immediately.

'Back to Salisbury Plain,' Alasdair complained to Fiona.

'I hope that's all it is,' she said miserably.

'You're not worried, are you darling?'

'Of course I'm worried, you fool.'

Her vehemence surprised him. 'You needn't be,' he advised. 'The people to worry about are all those poor miserable civilians who're being called up.'

'It's all right for you to talk,' Fiona retorted. 'I expect you look forward to a nice gory war. Well, just remember that I don't care if you never get a medal, as long as you come home.'

'I didn't know you cared so much,' he joked.

'Of course I care. I don't want to be a war widow.'

'Thanks. I thought you were worried about me.'

'Oh, Alasdair.' She held up her face for a kiss. 'I do worry about you,' she said a moment later. 'You know I do. I hate wars. They're such stupid things. Was anything better alfter the last war? Of course not, not a thing. I don't know what they think this one is going to accomplish, but when it's over I'll be surprised if we've gained anything. All we're likely to do is to double the national debt.'

Alasdair's mind was not on his family during those last days at home. Loring had already gone to France with his squadron, as part of the Air Component of the British Expeditionary Force. The 2nd Grampians, however, were destined for a quiet winter. They were detached from the Highland Division to which they properly belonged, and after two months on Salisbury Plain they found themselves in Edinburgh Castle. There they spent the rest of 1939, fretting and fuming. The 1st Battalion had gone straight from India to France where they swelled the ranks of the B.E.F.

Alasdair, strangely enough, took it all philosophically. Nothing was happening in France, anyway, and he was certain it was going to be a long and ferocious war. There was plenty of time.

A few days after the outbreak of the war, Lord Maurice Blood arrived at Grunaglack. In the same week Finvola gave up her job in England and returned to Ardclune House. Leona had not seen her sister for several years.

At thirty-two Finvola already had the pursed mouth and disapproving stare of a Victorian schoolma'am. Leona, who had often wondered why she had never married, wondered no longer.

'When is you husband going to join up?' Finvola asked her, on her second day home.

'Rajah join the Army, do you mean?' Leona laughed. 'He's got a job at the India Office. They wouldn't let him.'

'I'm sure anyone can write minutes on Government files. I would have thought he'd want to do his bit.'

Leona blinked at her sister.

'He'll do whatever is required of him,' she answered placidly, fighting down her temper.

'I've no doubt Gordon will stay in America, safe and sound,' Finvola sniffed.

'I wonder you don't expect Andrew to join up,' Leona retorted sarcastically.

'That isn't funny. I'm surprised at you. Andrew is a poor suffering soul. You should know better than to make fun of him.'

'I wasn't making fun of him,' Leona retorted testily, forbearing to add that she had been making fun of Finvola. It was plain that any sense of humour Finvola might once have possessed had disappeared entirely.

'I suppose Lord Maurice will shelter behind the coat-tails of the Foreign Secretary,' Finvola went on waspishly.

'I expect Maurice will do what he's told. I should think a trained and experienced diplomat might be worth more to the war effort than a totally untrained soldier.'

'It won't be thanks to people like you that we win the war,' Finvola snapped back.

'Tell me, just what did you do in London?' Leona asked sweetly.

'I was an organizer in Lifeline.'

'What's Lifeline?'

'How typical that you shouldn't know. We work mostly in the East End, around the docks, rescuing sailors.'

'Rescuing them from what?'

'From vice of course. I should have thought that was obvious.'

Leona tried to imagine the slim, sharp-featured Finvola rescuing some burly deckhand with a three-month thirst, and began to giggle. The expression on Finvola's face only made her giggle more. Luckily Janet came into the room.

'Hullo, darlings, what's the joke?' she asked.

'Leona seems to think that my work in London is a fit subject for childish laughter,' Finvola accused.

Leona looked beseechingly at her mother, unable to stop the giggles.

'Stop it, darling,' Janet told her casually.

'Sorry. I was trying to stop it. Only . . .' She began to giggle again.

'I shall go and look after Andrew,' Finvola stated firmly. 'I don't trust that nurse at all. There's no need for a nurse now that I'm home. I can give the poor boy the attention he needs.'

'Oh dear,' Janet said when she had flounced out of the room, 'I think I've just been put in my place.'

'She said,' Leona managed to stammer, 'that she rescued sailors from vice. In the East End. I could just picture it.'

'Yes, well I daresay it's very natural, but you shouldn't laugh at her, really you shouldn't, darling. Besides, if she does want to make a full-time job of Andrew it will be wonderful. I expect she's terribly efficient and capable.'

'Too terribly,' Leona agreed.

'What were you saying at breakfast about Rajah Sahib going away? I didn't follow.'

'He's leaving at the end of the week. He has to find a

small flat in London, then he'll come back for a final two weeks before he starts work. He's going to live in London by himself.'

'Is that fair to him?'

'You don't understand. I want to go with him but he won't hear of it. He insists that the children and I stay here with you.'

'I expect he's right,' Janet said slowly. 'It will be marvellous for your father and me, having you and Finvola, and the two children. When there were just the two of us and Andrew, life got us down sometimes.'

'I can't believe that.'

'I was only thinking of Rajah. It will be lonely for him.'

'I know. The poor dear will hate every minute of it,' Leona said with a shrug. 'It's the first time we've been separated for more than a night or two. I shall miss him.'

'Have you been happy?' Janet asked.

'Yes, terribly happy. You've no idea how splendid he is. Sometimes he puts on that pompous air, or else he becomes very quiet and won't talk, but when you really get to know him he isn't like that at all. He has a wonderful sense of fun. He's clever too.'

'I rather gathered that his C.S.I. was out of the ordinary.'

'It was the talk of India for a week or two. I don't know the details myself, for he won't discuss it, but I do know that it was because of his work that there weren't serious riots in Sialkot in 1934 and 1935. He didn't get any support from the Governor. The Viceroy was very pleased with him, and of course Maxton, the Governor, got a terrible rapping over it, and promptly spread the word around that Rajah is related to the Viceroy. They sent Maxton home eventually, but he got his knighthood and a fat pension, so it wasn't much of a punishment really.'

'I'm afraid I know nothing about the ins and outs of

the Indian Civil Service. I'm sure Rajah was a credit to it and to you. Poor man, going to London at a time like this. He may be bombed.'

Leona and Sir Lauchlan went round to Grunaglack House a few days later to see Lord Maurice. Susan insisted on taking Leona into her morning room while the two men went to the library. Leona would far rather have been with the men, but Susan had strong ideas on a woman's place in the house, and instead Leona had to listen to a lot of talk about children's ailments, the inconvenience of going to war, and how Susan had managed to get hold of six fifty-gallon drums of petrol for their new Daimler in case the Government rationed petrol.

Maurice sympathized with Lauchlan over his job in London.

'I expect I'll be off abroad again very soon,' Maurice said contentedly, lighting a fat cigar. 'They won't leave me in England for long. There's a whisper – nothing more mind you – that I'll be going to Washington. I'd like that. I'd feel safer if Susan and the children were on the other side of the Atlantic.'

'They'd go along would they?'

'I should think so. What's the point of staying here? Suppose there's an invasion?'

Sir Lauchlan frowned. A lot of people were going about saying, 'What if there's an invasion?' but they weren't running away. Was Blood running away? He had his job to do like anyone else.

'Nice work if you can get it,' he grunted.

'This war's going to play havoc with everything,' Maurice complained. 'Prices will shoot up, taxes will go up – it's absolute hell for anyone with a fixed income.'

'Have you got a fixed income?' Rajah asked, surprised.

'Yes. My father bought me an annuity when I was twenty-one. He did the same for my two brothers and my sister. Only my elder brother can weather the storm. All the land and the money will go to him. I daresay he'll make a packet out of the war. It's no fun being a younger son.'

'I see,' Lauchlan mused. He himself had inherited a few thousands with his title and that was all. There was a small house in Arisaig, which he had never sold. It was let to tenants who paid £10 a month to live in it. He thought it would be nice to have an annuity and a nice house.

'I've got two thousand a year, that's all,' Maurice said in a moment of unexpected expansiveness. 'Just two thousand plus my salary. It isn't much for a fellow with two sons to bring up. The trouble is that they tax it as unearned income.'

'That must be annoying.'

'It's worse. Sometimes we find it difficult to make ends meet. Luckily my father gives me money at Christmas and on my birthday, which they can't tax, but it's only five hundred.'

'Really.' Sir Lauchlan had to put his hand to his mouth. He had often wondered how the Bloods managed for money, since Susan had inherited nothing much. It was illuminating to learn of the hardships involved in being the younger son of what he had recently found out was one of Britain's wealthier Marquesses.

'I suppose you don't have these problems?' Maurice said casually.

'No.' Rajah Sahib shook his head and smiled. 'Thank God.'

It was true too. He had no money at all to speak of, and therefore no money problems. Leona had a very handsome allowance from Wee Ken, which was tax free and went up as the cost of living went up. In fact they didn't use her income much and managed quite well on his salary and his official allowances. Their tastes were much more modest than Susan's. Leona's money went into the bank as an insurance against the future.

He and Leona compared notes on the drive home.

'I feel sorry for Susan,' Leona said sympathetically.

'I can't think why, my dear.'

'Because her father was a spendthrift. He gave her expensive tastes and grand ideas but no money to support them. She's really very nice but she thinks it's clever to put on airs and have lots of servants she can't really afford and certainly doesn't need. Her trouble is that she's never got over Maurice being a lord, even if he's only one by courtesy.'

'Blood isn't snobbish,' Sir Lauchlan said pensively. 'He's got funny ideas on what constitutes poverty, but I wouldn't say he gives himself any airs or graces.'

'That's exactly it, darling. There's a tremendous difference between his father and Susan's.'

'True. Incidentally Maurice thinks he may be going to Washington. He said he'd take Susan and the children along.'

'That's odd. The way Susan was talking you'd think she intended to stay here all through the war.'

She told him about the petrol, and also how Susan was talking of buying crates of tinned food and stocking up the cellars at Grunaglack. She had already bought twenty-five dozen bottles of champagne.

'Champagne? What in God's name would anyone want with three hundred bottles of bubbly? Is it good stuff?'

'I don't know. She said she got it at a bargain price. Anyway, you know Susan.'

'My God, Blood is a long-suffering man. I love you, darling, but I can't answer for the consequences if you try to corner the market in champagne.'

She chuckled.

Maurice Blood's long-suffering attitude to his wife underwent a severe strain soon after this. The rumour was confirmed and he was told that he was being sent to Washington. He told Susan about it exultantly.

'You'll come with me of course, or would you rather follow?' he asked.

'I shan't come at all.'

'What?'

'I shan't come at all. I've bought this house and I intend to stay here with the boys. We're in no danger here.'

'You'd be far safer in the States. Anyway, I'm going aren't I?'

'That's your job.'

'You mean to say you refuse to come and live with me?'

'I'm not going to America while there's a war on. In fact I'm tired of living abroad. I was born here and I like it. What's the point of my buying the house if I'm not going to stay? Besides, think of all that petrol.'

'The petrol won't rot. Look here, you keep talking about buying this house, but it was my money.'

'Your money?' She gave him a scornful look. 'It's your duty to support your wife and that includes giving her a home. You got this place cheaply. You've no house of your own.'

'Nevertheless it isn't yours. I bought it for *us*.'

'All right then. You bought it for us, and I intend to stay in it. What's wrong with that? I'm quite happy to live in the home you've provided. It would be a trifle more gentlemanly if you didn't keep harping on the question of whose money it was.'

'Can't you see I'm going overseas?' he asked, exasperated. 'It's your duty to come with me. I bought this house as a place to spend our leaves and to retire to. Dammit, you can't expect me to spend the war in the States alone.'

'Why not? I'll be spending it alone here and it's far less exciting than Washington will be.'

'But I don't want you to stay here,' he exclaimed irritably. 'I want you to come with me.'

'I'm sorry. I wouldn't dream of taking the children across the Atlantic with a war on. Look what happened to the *Athenia*.'

The British liner *Athenia* had been sunk without warning by the U.30 on the day war was declared. Of one hundred and twelve lives lost off the Irish coast of Donegal, twenty-eight had been Americans. The Germans weren't fussy about whom they killed, it seemed. The war at sea had started without any loss of time.

'It isn't particularly dangerous,' he protested. 'A fast liner can outdistance any U-boat.'

'So you may say. I had no intention of putting it to the test, believe me.'

She stuck to her guns, much to Maurice's astonishment. It had never occurred to him that when she left him in Rome she was giving up the overseas career which he had embraced even before he met her. He had assumed that she was anxious to take over the house and put it in order for them; equally he had assumed that she would go abroad with him again on his next appointment.

By the end of the year Maurice was in Washington and Sir Lauchlan was at his desk in London. Leona, who found her sister Finvola insufferable most of the time, took to visiting Grunaglack as often as she could. She found Susan's pretentiousness more endurable than Finvola's carping, nagging and sniffing. Finvola, it had to be admitted, was a wonderful sister to Andrew. Janet was overjoyed and Wee Ken was impressed, and neither was very much amused when Leona pointed out that Andrew was simply a substitute for a drunken sailor. Kenneth in fact was rather hurt so Leona dropped the subject. It was one fight she could not win. Finvola had taken over with a vengeance.

At Castlemore Fiona kept herself busy with her two children, and she and Norma knitted balaclava helmets and socks, as did so many other women throughout the length and breadth of Britain. Alasdair was safe in Edinburgh Castle, and to the uninitiated it seemed that the Maginot Line in France was effectively keeping the Germans at bay until the B.E.F. and the French Army were ready to advance and capture Berlin. Norma had put up a framed map on the wall of the drawing room, which was hardly used nowadays, and on it were little red pins showing the allied dispositions. She referred to the room, jokingly, as the War Room, and took much heart from looking at the map.

It wasn't very far to Berlin, not on the map. She was sure everything would be all right this time. It wasn't like the first war with millions of men in trenches shooting one another and dying in the mud.

This was a much nicer war.

*

5

In April Boy Loring won the D.F.C. His squadron was at Vassincourt, about a hundred and thirty miles east of Paris. He had a score of five already when he attacked a formation of twelve German aircraft near Metz, shot down two and damaged three more before being shot himself. He managed to crash land near Rouvres, where there was another R.A.F. squadron, and got away with only scratches. The newspapers carried the story on the front pages, for at that stage of the war news was news, and there were precious few heroes to write about.

Norma wrote immediately to May, who was now working in the library at Chichester. May's reply was very restrained. Norma understood.

'It must be a terrific strain on her,' she said to Fiona at lunch on the day May's letter arrived. 'It's bad enough having someone in the Army, but in the R.A.F. they can be off fighting for their lives and then be back home for lunch. The strain is continuous. Thank goodness Alasdair is still in Edinburgh.'

In fact Alasdair was nowhere near Edinburgh, although they did not know it. Normally he wrote to Fiona once a week, and he was almost a week overdue. She did not realize that the 2nd Grampians were in Norway, where they had been sent to reinforce an infantry brigade under General Carton de Wiart. They withdrew from Norway early in June after the evacuation of Narvik. While the world held its breath during Dunkirk, as almost an entire Army was lifted off the French beaches and brought home in safety, Fiona and Norma took comfort from the fact that Alasdair was safe in Scotland. A letter – which had been posted by a friend after they had left Edinburgh – reached Fiona in mid-May. Alsadair said he was extremely busy and couldn't write much for a week or two. Another of the same sort arrived during Dunkirk.

At the height of Dunkirk, Alasdair and a company of Grampians in Norway held up a German advance for six hours before extricating themselves with twelve killed and twenty-two wounded. Alasdair rather enjoyed the excitement of it, and was sorry when they were forced to leave Norway and return to Scotland. He would have liked to stay on. He was given leave and was actually sitting in the garden with Norma and Fiona when the press in Inverness telephoned Norma. The list of awards had been published and they had picked out Alasdair's name. He had won the Military Cross and they wanted to know if his mother had a photograph of him.

'You can come and take one,' she said, her mind in a whirl. 'He's at home.'

'Is he on leave?'

'Yes.'

'Then we will send a photographer tomorrow. Will that be all right?'

'Yes of course.' Then she asked the question which puzzled her. 'Are you sure he was at Dunkirk?'

'Dunkirk, Mrs MacInnes? I didn't say that. Your son was in Norway. He held up the German Army for six hours. Didn't you know?'

'No, until you phoned I thought he was in Edinburgh, at the Castle.'

The news editor grinned to himself. That would make a good human touch to the story. 'While his mother thought he was safely in Edinburgh Castle, Captain Alasdair MacInnes of the Royal Grampian Highlanders was holding up a German advance in Norway for six hours.' Oh yes, the story would write itself. It was worth at least six inches plus a photograph.

'Everything all right?' Fiona asked as Norma came and sat down beside them and poured more tea.

'Yes thank you. Tell me, Alasdair, how is Edinburgh? Are the shops busy?'

'I think so. I didn't go shopping much.'

'Did you have a wet spell two weeks ago?'

'I don't know. Yes, I believe we did. I never notice the weather much.'

'It would be difficult to notice it all the way from Norway, wouldn't it?'

'What's that?' Fiona asked, pricking up her ears as Alasdair bit his lip. What's this about Norway?'

'Ask him,' Norma said accusingly.

'Well, we were only there for a few weeks. How did you find out? I'd arranged for someone to post a couple of letters for me. I would have written anyway, but we came home again so quickly.'

'The newpaper has been on the telephone. You won the Military Cross.'

'Did I really? Are you sure?' Alasdair suddenly showed interest.

'Yes. They're coming tomorrow to take your photograph.'

79

'Oh dash it, couldn't we just send them a snapshot? I don't want the press here.'

'You're going to have them. He held up the German Army for six hours, Fiona. That's what they say.'

'Not all by myself I didn't,' Alasdair protested. 'I was in charge, that's all.'

'All that time we were listening to the news from France and thinking how nice it was that you were safe in Edinburgh,' Fiona said accusingly. 'Alasdair, how could you?'

'We left in a hurry you see, as reinforcements for Carton de Wiart. Besides, what could I say in a letter except that I was going away, and then you'd have worried?'

'Do you think we won't worry in future?' Fiona demanded hotly.

'What's there to worry about? We're out of Norway and out of Europe. We don't seem to be doing at all well, but at least we're safe at home.'

'It hasn't taken you long to follow in your father's footsteps, has it?' Norma asked, not altogether angrily. She was proud of her son.

'It was pure luck. The Germans thought that there was at least a battalion of us, but there was only one company. We fooled them beautifully.'

'I'm sure you enjoyed it,' Fiona said stiffly.

'You mustn't worry about me, darling,' Alasdair said gently. 'It doesn't do any good.'

She sighed and gave him a rueful smile. 'I suppose you're right. I shall be glad when this war's over.'

It was something they were all to say many times in the year which lay ahead.

On Friday the 5th of July 1940 Wee Ken and Janet were driving into Fort William, leaving Finvola in charge of Andrew. Leona had gone to visit some friends in Inverness. The Local Defence Volunteer force was in the process of being turned into the Home Guard and

Wee Ken had been invited to accept a commission. The idea of getting into uniform again amused him, and he was on his way to find out more about it and what it would involve. Just outside the village of Coruanan an oncoming lorry went out of control and hit them head on. The lorry driver and his mate were uninjured. Kenneth and Janet died instantly.

The shock of the tragedy seemed to paralyse the whole family except Finvola. She organized everything with her usual brisk efficiency. For Norma it was a sad blow. Wee Ken was the last of Merchant Bob's five fine sons. Alasdair and Donald had died in the First World War, Bobbie had been killed in a similar sort of car accident early in 1936, and Charles had died in Paris at Easter, 1938. Now, that Ken and Janet had gone too, she was the sole survivor of happier days, and she sat in the sitting room staring out over the fountain towards the loch, seeing ghostly figures from the past walking among the trees and the flowers. It was ridiculous, she thought. She was fifty-five, that was all – far too young to be a sole survivor. She could recall that Christmas of 1906 so clearly, when she and her parents had come to Castlemore from Beauly to celebrate her engagement to Donald, the third son – that Christmas when she had met Dair, and all the previous plans went for nothing as she and Dair fell wildly in love. They had all gone, including Charles's first two wives – she didn't count Vivienne, the third, who was French and who was a total stranger living in Paris – plus Alison Mathieson, who had made Bobbie so happy, and now Janet. It seemed these years as though nothing but misfortune was in store for the family. Who would have thought, thirty-five years ago, that there would be only two male MacInneses left in the country, one her own son now away serving in the Army, risking his life, and the other a child of five, not yet six? Apart from them there was Gordon and his infant son in America, Dougal and his son Torquil in Spain, and lastly poor Andrew, poor mad Andrew at Ardclune. If anything happened to Alasdair Beg it would leave only the child, Pal Al. The others could be forgotten. They counted for nothing.

Fiona found her and put an arm round her.

'Can I get you anything, Norma?'

'No, my dear, nothing thank you. I'm just being miserable.'

'I've telephoned Miss Weir's. If we send Inglis for Deirdre he can bring her home for the funeral, and she needn't go back. They break up in ten days' time for the summer.'

'That was thoughtful of you. Will you tell Inglis?'

'Yes, of course. We've just about got enough petrol.'

'Good. I wonder what sort of will Wee Ken left.'

'We'll be able to find out after the funeral. Finvola has invited us all to be present at the reading and to stay to tea.'

'Has she?' Norma mustered a smile. 'Finvola should join the Waafs or the Wrens. She'd make a good officer.'

Fiona smiled back. 'According to Leona, she wouldn't be missed at Ardclune if she did just that.'

The funeral was held in Fort William on the Tuesday morning. There was a remarkably large turnout because Wee Ken had made many friends in the county over the years. He wasn't an ostentatious man, but in his own quiet way he had a large circle of acquaintances and everyone liked him. Afterwards the family adjourned to Ardclune where Finvola dispensed sherry and fruit cake.

When the will was read it was found that in the event of Janet's death Wee Ken had left his money in four equal shares, Andrew's to be put in trust and the income used to provide him with whatever nursing he would need in his unfortunate life. Ardclune, however, was left to Finvola. The will had stipulated, of course, that Andrew must be looked after at Ardclune and not sent away unless under explicit doctor's orders. This presented no difficulty as Finvola enjoyed caring for her brother.

Finvola succeeded in taking the wind out of Leona's sails when the others had all left and they were alone in the sitting room.

'You'll be welcome to stay on here of course, Leona.'

'I beg your pardon?' Leona was puzzled.

'I said, you and the children will be welcome to stay here. I would like you to look upon Ardclune as home while you husband is away in London.'

Leona swallowed hard. She had never looked upon it as anything else. She had not really taken in the fact that Finvola was now the owner and that she was Finvola's guest.

'Thank you,' she replied feebly.

'There's just one thing.'

'Yes?'

'Eve and Mary. They're charming children but they're just a little noisy, especially first thing in the morning. I've spoken to them once or twice already. If you could persuade them to be a little more quiet . . .'

'Yes,' Leona stammered. 'Of course.'

Finvola gave her a wintry smile.

It was from that time that Leona's friendship with Susan began to flourish, against all probabilities. Finvola was an uncongenial companion and Susan was in a similiar plight with two small children to bring up and a husband abroad. Admittedly Sir Lauchlan was only in London and would be able to get up to Scotland twice a year, but their circumstances were very much the same.

At the end of July, May wrote that Boy Loring had been promoted to Squadron Leader and given a squadron of his own. He was at Biggin Hill in Kent, and his new squadron had Spitfires instead of Hurricanes. The Battle of Britain was entering its most intense period and May was living under constant strain. In August Loring was awarded the Distinguished Service Order, and his personal score now stood at twenty-two confirmed victories. Halfway through September the battle was virtually over as the Germans switched targets, and early in October Hitler cancelled Operation Sealion, his invasion of Britain.

Rather to Norma's surprise, May said she and her husband were coming to Castlemore for a week. Alasdair happened to be on leave at the same time, so the old house became quite lively for a few days, marred only by the fact that Alasdair's was embarkation leave. He was going overseas. Officially his destination was secret, but he himself had no doubt that the 2nd Grampians were bound for the Western Desert. He had been lucky, there was no denying the fact. The 1st Battalion had been with the Highland Division, serving under French orders, when they had been trapped at St Valery-en-Caux. The whole divison had been either killed or captured. It did not return from France. They were the unfortunate ones for whom there was no Dunkirk. A new 51st Highland Division would be formed, and a new 1st Battalion of the Royal Grampian Highlanders would be raised, but for those who had gone to France with the old 1st in the B.E.F. the war was over already.

Alasdair talked to Loring about the Battle of Britain. He knew very little except what had been released by the propaganda machine which claimed phenomenal successes and boasted of Britain's superiority. Unlike Germany Britain did not tell lies, did not often conceal defeats and reverses, and did not really deliberately distort the truth very much. On the other hand the purpose of propaganda is to boost morale and that, like all forms of salesmanship, consists of crying aloud the value of one's wares and their superiority to other goods.

Boy Loring was rather angry about the impression most people had of the battle.

'There's so much rot talked,' he said impatiently as he and Alasdair sat one evening having a drink before dinner. 'We're supposed to have been better than the Germans.'

'Weren't you?'

'As pilots? As men? I don't think so. They've got some terrific people. Listen, Alasdair, we didn't win an offensive, we beat off an attack. The chaps did bloody magnificently. Nobody believed we could hold them off and we did, and if anyone wants to say "good show chaps" to us, I'm all in favour, but do let's stick to the facts. Think of the German handicap. We have a radar system, we could see the attacks building up and pick out the feints from the real thing. If the Germans had really gone all out against the radar masts, instead of the half-hearted little attacks they made, we'd have been in trouble. For that the German leaders take the blame. There's another thing, we were fighting on home territory, the battle was on our doorstep. I've made as many as six sorties in a day, but the Germans had to fly a long way just to get to the fight so their time over target was limited by fuel. If they were shot down they were made prisoner whereas lots of our chaps were shot down in the morning and flew again the same day. I did it myself.'

'Did you?'

'May doesn't know, but yes, three times. Once I crash-landed and twice I baled out. The Germans couldn't do that. We lost far more planes then we did pilots. We had the advantage. Even if we came down in the Channel we had a good chance of being picked up by our own people. Everything was in our favour, including the aircraft. The job of the Hurricanes was to go for the bombers and the Hurricanes could make mincemeat of them. Our job in the Spits was to sit up above them and keep the German escort fighters off. The Spit has the edge on the Me 109, and even on the 110. The Germans put up a bloody good show, and it doesn't flatter us to hear people talk as though the Germans were second-rate fliers in second-rate machines. Their bombers were vulnerable but it was a close-run thing with their fighters. In the end they were betrayed.'

'How do you mean?' Alasdair asked, interested.

'Goering switched targets away from the airfields. They wanted to knock out the R.A.F. and if they'd kept at it for another two weeks they'd have brought us to our knees, quite literally. I know I had the shakes and so did most of my chums. Things were getting pretty desperate when suddenly the whole thing changed and they started bombing London. I'm not belittling what we did – I saw too many good types get the chop, boys we cannot re-place – it's just that I don't like the official ballyhoo. We were damned lucky over the radar and the changing of the targets. Another thing, one day we'll be attacking Germany. Our bombers will be going over there in day-light and I'll be flying escort on them. I hope I can put up as good a show as the Germans when that happens, with a permanent worry about fuel and the knowledge that if I come down I'll be put in the bag by Jerry.'

'I see. You'd better not say anything to May and Fiona about this.'

'Of course I won't,' Boy laughed. 'Not damned likely. There's another thing, while I'm on the subject. Losses of our own aircraft and pilots are probably fairly accurate, but I'm not sure our estimate of German losses is. It's hard to see exactly what's going on in a dogfight and often several aircraft attack one Jerry. I've got a feeling our claims are too high. We shan't know till after the war. Anyway, we're all glad of the rest, I can tell you.'

'What happens to you next?' Alasdair asked.

'Who can say? I hope they don't send us overseas, not for a bit yet. May and I are trying to add to the family and I'd like to be around till it happens.'

Alasdair nodded and smiled. He rather liked this brother-in-law of his, and he certainly had a refreshingly frank view of life. It would be fun getting to know him properly after the war.

Alasdair and the battalion arrived in North Africa early in November, in time to take part in General O'Connor's desert offensive against the Italians. His letters home were not very frequent and never eloquent. Fiona was accustomed to his stilted, inhibited, unsatisfactory notes. She found it difficult to remember her husband as clearly as she would like. Often she went for hours without giving him so much as a thought. This characteristic never ceased to trouble her. It made her feel both heartless and disloyal.

That Christmas a new distraction came into their lives. There was a new unit, some sort of secret establishment, at Lochailort, a few miles west of Castlemore, at the head of Loch Ailort. Norma invited some of the officers on the staff of the unit to come to Castlemore on Christmas Day, and six of them arrived. Susan could not come because she had some sort of party of her own, and Leona was spending a depressing Christmas with Finvola. She had hoped that Sir Lauchlan would get to Ardclune but he hadn't been able to leave London. What would have been a very dull Christmas at Castlemore turned into rather a gay affair and they even danced an eightsome reel.

Their guests were all interesting. Although at that time they did not know it, Lochailort was a Commando school. The staff came from all sorts of unusual peacetime occupations and were a tough but high-spirited crowd. Deirdre, on holiday from school, made quite a hit with one of the younger officers, much to Norma's amusement. Deirdre was sixteen now and a real beauty.

The staff at Castlemore had been depleted by the war. Fraser the footman and Inglis the chauffeur had both been called up. MacOmie the gardener had surprised everyone by going off and joining the Merchant Navy. Norma's maid, Jean, had left to go to Aberdeen to look after her mother who now lived there alone. Even so they had four servants left and considered themselves very fortunate. The Rolls-Royce was sold and they made do with Betty's little car which was quite sufficient for their needs, so the loss of Inglis was not important to them.

Norma made gardening her hobby. She had always been fussy about the appearance of the Castlemore grounds, and with no gardener the situation was serious. In addition she had greatly enlarged the vegetable garden. They would grow all their own vegetables and a little fruit. Rather reluctantly Fiona helped her. She was not enamoured by the mechanics of gardening although she enjoyed the end product as much as anyone. The days slid past quickly, and they were hardly aware of the passage of time.

In April Andrew died at Ardclune. He slipped away peacefully in his sleep one evening and no one was sorry to see him go. He had never had a normal life and he had made things extremely difficult for everyone else. Exactly a month later Squadron Leader Robert Loring, D.S.O., D.F.C., A.F.C., R.A.F., crashed into a hillside at night and died instantly. In her letter to Norma, May said she was returning to her cottage in Weobley which had been lying empty, and that she would try to get her old job back. Norma urged her to return home to Castlemore, but May refused adamantly. Norma could not understand it, but Fiona thought that perhaps she could. May would want to be alone for a time. Sympathy often only served to keep wounds open. Fiona wrote to Alasdair and told him about Boy Loring. It crossed an exultant letter from him saying that he had been awarded a bar to his Military Cross.

She sat in her room puzzling over the letter. Medals were the subject of congratulations, of course, but Alasdair had such a childish delight in his. It was as though he felt his whole purpose in life was to win medals. She remembered how he had fretted in India when he was in garrison instead of out on patrol. One of the things she had admired in him when she had met him first had been his enthusiasm for the Army, but she had not known how irritating it might become. Didn't he realize that it upset her to think of him in danger? Certainly he didn't win medals for living safely. The worst of it was that she couldn't share her thoughts with Norma who was proud to see her son following in his father's footsteps. She lived in constant fear that he would be killed like his father, but this did not diminish her pride in him. Fiona wished she could develop Norma's philosophic attitude. The difference between them was that she, Fiona, wished with all her heart that Alasdair was not in the Army at all, whereas Norma merely prayed for his safety.

Norma knew nothing of Fiona's anguish, for anguish it was. The first flush of love had faded to be replaced only by fears, uncertainties and the horrible suspicion that heroes were really only sheep sacrificed on the altar of political expediency and stupidity. How could she say what she felt when the whole country applauded Winston Churchill's speeches egging them on to fight to the last man for the sake of civilisation? Norma was a great admirer of Churchill.

Pal Al, now five and a half, was being brought up by Norma on a strict diet of hero worship. Norma's fierce pride in her dead husband and fighting son communicated itself easily to the child, and his most prized possession was a photograph of his father complete with basket-hilted claymore, wearing the ribbon of the M.C. It was quite natural, but Fiona found herself leaving Pal Al more and more to his grandmother's care, and turning to her daughter, the bubbling, joyous child she had named Frances Mary. The two and a half year old girl adored her mother and toddled about the house in Fiona's wake, talking happily to herself.

One day in June Susan arrived at Castlemore, white-faced. Norma had not seen much of Susan. Indeed the last time she had visited Grunaglack had been in January when she had learned that Gordon's wife, Annabelle, had died in America. It had been a wretched affair by all accounts. It seemed Annabelle drank, and she and Gordon had had a party on New Year's Eve. Next morning Annabelle had fallen out of an open window on to a concrete path below. It needn't have killed her but she had landed on her head and broken her neck. Gordon's letter to his sister had been distraught and full of self-recrimination. Susan had been horrified at the picture it revealed. If she thought of Annabelle at all, it was as the expensively-reared daughter of a millionaire from the upper crust of American society. Now her brother Gordon was blaming himself for letting his wife drink too much on New Year's Eve. In Susan's well-planned world no one drank too much. They drank certain drinks at certain times because it was the proper thing to do.

It would be misleading to say that Susan saw Norma as a mother. Susan didn't really know very much about having a mother, nor did she care. Norma, however, was the senior member of the family now, the one to whom they all turned in times of stress. As Norma embraced her she began to cry.

'Susan, what's the matter? Come this way.'

She led Susan into the sitting room and made her sit down. She was dabbing at her eyes with a handkerchief.

'It's Gordon,' she said with a catch in her voice.

'Is he in trouble?'

'Worse. He's dead.'

'Gordon dead? But he's only, what – thirty-five?'

'Yes, his birthday was last month. Oh, Norma, he's committed suicide.'

Norma stared aghast. Susan fumbled in her handbag and produced a bulky letter.

'Here,' she said, 'it's from old Gideon Fairfax.'

Stunned, Norma skimmed through the letter which Fairfax had written to Gordon's sister. It was brutal in places. Gordon had been drinking heavily since Annabelle's death. The marriage had been unhappy for the past year or more. Annabelle drank too much anyway and Gordon, to put it bluntly, had other women, and one fed the other, so that it was a vicious double circle. Gordon had taken an overdose of sleeping pills and it was all over now. The Fairfax family would take care of the children, Jean and Charles, and bring them up as their own. He was very sorry, but Gordon had been going downhill rapidly and it was better this way.

'Did you know of this?' Norma asked Susan.

'No, only what we both knew at the time of Annabelle's death – that she drank a lot. I didn't know that they had been unhappy or that Gordon was behaving so badly. Oh dear.'

Norma went to a cupboard and produced a bottle and glasses. She poured two whiskies and added a little soda water from a siphon. She handed the larger one to Susan who drank it and shuddered as the fiery spirit went down. Then Norma rang and ordered coffee.

'Poor Susan,' she said sympathetically. 'I suppose the best thing will be to leave the two children there in America.'

'Yes. It's all so vulgar.'

'What?' Norma wondered if she misheard.

'Gordon – having affairs with other women.'

'Men do you know my dear, especially unhappy ones; even women do, come to that.'

'Only the lower classes.'

Norma bit her lip and walked to the window. Sometimes she wondered if Susan was completely sane. Did she honestly believe the lower classes had a monopoly on vice? Norma was conservative to the core, but she suspected that the upper classes were far more vicious – they had much more time and money.

'How am I to hold up my head again?' Susan complained.

'Who's to know?' Norma asked coldly. 'Even Maurice

needn't know. All you have to do is to say that Gordon died.'

'Of what?'

'Anything you like. Gideon Fairfax isn't going to write letters to other people. He's told you and that's all he'll do.'

'That's right.' Susan brightened. 'I could say that Gordon died of tuberculosis.'

'I shouldn't do that, it isn't at all sudden. Say he developed cerebral meningitis and dropped dead. That's far more plausible.'

'Of course. Thank you Norma. I knew I could rely on you. You won't tell anyone will you?'

'Not outside the family.'

'Not *anyone*.'

'I don't know. I'll have to think about that. I shan't contradict you if you say anything different, anyway."

'I don't want people to know.'

'To know what? That your brother was human? That he was miserable?'

'I'd rather keep quiet about the whole affair. Cerebral meningitis is much better.'

'Suit yourself.'

'He doesn't say if Gordon left any money.'

'His children would be his heirs.'

'He might have left something to me, his sister.'

'You'd better write to Gideon Fairfax.'

'I shall. He's a millionaire. What's money to a man like that?'

Norma bit back her natural retort. She suspected that Gideon Fairfax would give Susan short shrift, and she doubted strongly if Gordon had made any provision in his will for Lady Maurice Blood!

'Have you shown this letter to Leona?' she asked suddenly, knowing how close Susan and Leona had become.

'No, not even to Leona. Only to you. Please keep my secret Norma.'

'Very well, I'll do my best. I don't think it is a subject that will be much discussed anyway. Gordon was pretty much a stranger here.'

'Thank God for that. How could he do anything so wicked?'

'As what? His girl friends or his suicide?'

'It's not funny,' Susan snapped, spots of colour showing on her cheeks.

They drank their coffee and then Susan drove off back to Grunaglack, there to write to tell her husband the bad news about her brother's sudden meningitis.

The same afternoon an Army jeep arrived at Castlemore bringing two officers. Fiona, who was walking in the garden, hurried up to it as it halted by the front of the house. She recognized the driver at once as Captain Edmonds from Lochailort.

'Hullo, Mrs MacInnes,' he greeted her brightly, swinging himself out of the jeep. He touched his cap in a sketchy salute. 'I've brought a friend along, Lieutenant Windsor.'

'How do you do,' Fiona said politely. She was wearing a dirndl skirt and carrying a basket of flowers. Her face was a little flushed and her eyes were bright. Lieutenant Windsor, tall, slim, dark-haired, looked at her closely and smiled.

'How do you do,' he replied in a firm, musical voice. 'We're interrupting.'

'No, honestly, I'd picked all the flowers I wanted. I was going to ask for some tea to be sent out. Will you both join me?'

'A pleasure,' Captain Edmonds agreed with alacrity.

Ipla had appeared in the doorway so Fiona gave her the basket of flowers, the trowel and the gardening gloves, and ordered tea. Then they walked towards the summer house.

'What brings you here, Captain?' she asked.

'An invitation. We're having a little party at the Mess

on Saturday, drinks and buffet lunch, to pay back some hospitality rather belatedly. Colonel Ewyas sent me round to invite you and Mrs MacInnes senior to come along, your guests too if you have any.'

'No guests,' Fiona laughed. 'Just Norma and myself. I'd be delighted and I'm sure Norma will be too.'

'It's a bit short notice but we've only just decided to have the party. Unexpected supplies of booze have arrived, including some champagne. It will be quite a decent party with lots of food. We're having it out of doors.'

'It sounds just marvellous. Ah, here's Norma now.'

Norma joined them and was introduced to Windsor and told about the party. She too said that she would like to attend. They all had tea together and Fiona turned her attention to the newcomer.

'Have you been at Lochailort long?' she asked.

'A whole week,' he laughed.

'I hope you'll like it. We know quite a number of the officers and it seems to be a happy place.'

'Mad,' Windsor laughed. 'That's what they are – all as mad as hatters. I shall enjoy it enormously. The Army was beginning to erode me.'

'What?'

'Erode me. Wear me down.'

'You don't approve of it?' she asked with a smile. 'Why did you join?

'I didn't want to get drowned and I didn't want to crash ten thousand feet onto the ground, so I had little option.'

'What were you doing before?'

'I was a journalist.'

'Was it interesting?'

'Yes, I thought so. I worked on *The Daily World*. I covered sport. It was rather fun being paid for doing what I would gladly have paid them to do.'

'No wonder you don't like the war.'

'Does anyone?'

94

She smiled, and thought of Alasdair. 'What's your first name?' she asked.

'Norman.'

'Norman Windsor? Shouldn't I know you? That sounds very familiar.'

'Not unless you're interested in climbing.'

'Of course! Mountaineering.'

He smiled. 'I'm surprised you've heard. Are you a climber?'

'Goodness no, but I do read the newpapers. You were quite famous.'

'Hardly that, but I did take part in one or two good expeditions.'

She looked at him with fresh interest, noting the broad shoulders, the steady look in his eyes, his strong hands. She knew Lochailort was a special unit and that they were a very tough bunch. Lieutenant Norman Windsor would be able to hold his own among them.

'You have a lovely home here,' he said, looking around.

'It is nice, isn't it?'

'What do you do with yourself?'

'Nothing much. I've been working a lot in the garden.'

'I love gardening,' he told her. 'It's nice and peaceful.'

'Do you have a garden at home?'

'Yes, my father is mad on flowers.'

'Where is home?'

'A place called Market Drayton in Shropshire.'

'You're a long way away here.'

'I know, I'm a long way from many things. James said on the way over that your husband is out in North Africa with the Army. Is that right?'

'Yes, he is.'

'What did he do before the war?'

'He's a regular.'

'Oh dear. I hope I haven't put my foot in it. I'm a bit irreverent about the military machine – amateur's privilege.'

95

'That's all right, you didn't say anything.'

'I hope not.'

'Please stop worrying,' she laughed. 'Tell me, what are you going to do after the war?'

'I don't know. I'd like to go abroad to America or Canada if I can. I'll write of course, that's my job, but not sport. I'll be out of touch so it would be a good time to change. I'd like to write freelance articles, topical ones, perhaps humorous. We'll see when the time comes.'

'That sounds rather fun.'

'Life is fun, don't you think? Not in the Army of course, which is idiotic. Oh dear, I've done it again.'

James Edmonds, who had been deep in conversation with Norma, leaned across.

'What's he up to? He's a bit of a heretic.'

'We were talking about what he'd do after the war,' Fiona smiled.

'Blow up Parliament, I'd guess,' Edmonds laughed. 'Norman's one of the world's rebels.'

Fiona waited a few moments and then asked the tall Lieutenant,

'Are you a rebel?'

'I suppose so.'

'I'm glad.'

He looked at her in surprise. She was not at all like a regular Army wife.

6

It had been a magnificent buffet lunch out of doors in front of the Officers' Mess. There was a crowd of local notables and Norma met a number of old friends. Fiona was the centre of a small group of commando officers for a while, but Norman Windsor managed to persuade her to come with him to the buffet table and afterwards a little way off on their own. It was a cloudless summer day, warm and brilliantly sunny.

'One would never dream there was a war on,' Fiona said wistfully, 'except for all you men in uniform. On days like this, war seems a crime.'

'It is a crime,' Norman replied. 'A hideous unforgivable crime. My father was in the last lot, and now I'm in this one. It makes me wonder if there is any point in marrying and having children. What for? So that they can go off to the next war?'

'Will there be another war?' she wondered.

'Hasn't there always been one, sooner or later? You don't believe all that 1914 rubbish about the war to end wars, do you? At least they are sparing us that sort of clap-trap this time. Have you any children?'

'Two. A boy nearly six and a girl almost three.'

'Doesn't it worry you?' Norman Windsor asked.

'Another war you mean? I'm far too busy worrying about this one.'

'Your husband's in the thick of it. It must worry you.'

'It does.'

'Sometimes I wish I had the sheer courage to be a conscientious objector.'

'You don't mean that,' Fiona told him lightly.

'Perhaps not, but they do have a courage of their own.'

'Were you at university?' she asked.

'Yes, three years at Oxford. That's when I became a confirmed climber.'

'Climbing in and out of college?' she asked with a laugh. 'Did you get a degree?'

'I read honours history and scraped through by the skin of my teeth. I don't think degrees are important.'

'I believe you're a cynic.'

'Sometimes I think I am,' he said mildly. 'It's a mad world and I don't like it all all. How can I put it? Everyone dresses up the truth to try to make whatever it is they're doing sound important. It's all a sham, all a gigantic confidence trick. That's why I want to write – to pull away all the camouflage and show the world for what it really is. It's not a bad place if you can glimpse it underneath the layers of pretence.'

'That sounds exciting.' Her eyes sparkled as she spoke.

'Do you think so?'

'Oh yes. That's worth while.'

'You know, I believe you understand me. Not many people do.'

'They wouldn't, and they wouldn't want to.'

'Right,' he agreed, laughing with her. 'How funny. I mean, you're an Army wife, a professional one. You're the last sort of person I expected to find myself talking to.'

'I married my husband, not the Army.'

'You're an exception then. I haven't met many regular wives, but I detest them.'

'Aren't you being a little bit unfair?' she asked. 'You've nothing in common with them, but don't detest them. They're just women, like any others, who took men for better or worse'

'I am rebuked,' he said lightly.

'No you aren't. I can't imagine you in a regular Army setting, and it's true that it can be deadly dull.'

'How does your husband stick it?'

98

'He was in India before the war, chasing tribesmen up and down the Khyber Pass.'

'Ah, stern stuff. Perhaps he's different – some are. Tell me, how did you like the peacetime Army?'

'I wasn't in it. I was here at Castlemore.'

'Even while your husband was in India?' he asked, astonished.

'We were married on the 18th of April 1934 and on the 14th of May we sailed for India. I came back in March the following year. I was ill and the doctors insisted I come home.'

'You certainly don't look ill now.'

'I'm not. It was quite mysterious and stopped the moment I set foot on the boat.'

'Psychosomatic.'

'What's that?'

'You imagined it,' he laughed.

'I most certainly did not, nor did the doctor. It took me quite a long time to get back my strength. The sickness left me very weak. Anyway I didn't have to stand too much station life and I must be honest and confess I loathed every second of it. It's far worse for wives than for the husbands. The men have got their work and some of them, like Alasdair, enjoy the Army.'

'You've made me think,' he said.

'In what way?'

'I've always said that only a moron would subject himself to peacetime soldiering, and I'm sure you'd never marry a moron, so I must be wrong.'

'You're inclined to be rather sweeping in your denunciations,' she smiled. 'That's all. They aren't all morons, believe me, but it does take a certain sort of mentality. There's a lot of drabness about soldiering and you have to be prepared to put up with that.'

'I'm just not one of nature's warriors,' he chuckled.

'What does your father do?'

'He's a doctor. We live in a rather quaint house called

99

Meadowbank just outside Market Drayton, and life was very pleasant till this stupid war began.'

'Back to the war.'

'Will you tell me how to get away from it?' he demanded.

'I might even do that,' she told him playfully.

'How?'

'Can you get away from here? Do you have a car or something?'

'I can get away sometimes, but transport is not so easy. I know, I can borrow a bicycle and cycling would keep me fit. Where do I go?'

'Not far. Meet me halfway to Castlemore, at the top of Loch Eilt. It isn't far. There's a little track runs round the end of the loch, to the south. I'll come on a bicycle too. I know a simply lovely picnic spot and you win a special prize if the war never enters your head while you're there. I don't think it will.'

'Why are you going to be on a cycle?' he asked.

'We must be discreet. I'm married, remember? Still, I would like a picnic and to be with someone who won't mention the war.'

'I'll be in uniform . . . no I won't. I'll manage to change on the way. I'll borrow something. This sounds wonderful. When is it to be?'

'Tomorrow of course, unless you have parades or whatever it is you do on Sundays.'

'We hardly ever have parades and I'm free all day tomorrow. I'll meet you whenever you say.'

'At ten in the morning. We'll make a day of it. It will be a change for both of us.'

'It certainly will.' He gave her a searching look. 'Are you serious?'

'Why shouldn't I be?'

'You're married, you hardly know me, it doesn't seem likely that you'd want my company.'

'You're too modest, and anyway we both hate the war

and we're going to stop it for one day. There's nothing sinister about that.'

'You know, I'm glad I met you,' he told her.

'I'm glad I met you too,' Fiona agreed. 'Now we'd better get back. People will be talking. This is a gossipy part of the world.'

She was right about that, for Norma, when she managed to get her alone, said rather reluctantly, 'Fiona, I don't think you should have spent quite so long with that young Lieutenant – what's his name? Windsor?'

'Norman Windsor. I found him very interesting. He's the mountaineer you know. You must have heard of him.'

'I haven't heard of him at all. I'm not suggesting that there was anything wrong, just that people do talk and you are married, aren't you?'

'Yes,' Fiona acknowledged with a laugh. 'He's quite safe with me.'

Norma smiled. 'That's not what I meant and you know it. Now let's change the subject.'

Neat, Fiona thought on as they drove home. Norma had done it beautifully – the reproach without reproach – then she decided that that was really clever and she must tell Norman. Still, word-play apart, it had been a reproach, and she was more acutely aware of the fact that she wasn't free at all. She wasn't quite sure what she thought of the situation.

Next morning she wondered if she hadn't been foolish. She got up very early and raided the pantry. She had concealed quite a lot of food before Mrs MacDonald found her ferreting about among the biscuits. Fiona explained airily that she was going out for the day and was making up a picnic. It was only later that Mrs MacDonald found time to be surprised at the amount of food Mistress Fiona seemed to have taken with her. Explaining it to Norma was more difficult, for Fiona had never gone away for a whole day before, and on a bicycle too. She said she was feeling caged and wanted to get away into the sunshine by herself. Norma appeared to accept the explanation and, feeling rather foolish, Fiona set off at last towards Lochailort and Arisaig.

When she reached the head of Loch Eilt, Norman stepped out on to the road from among some bushes.

'Good morning,' he called.

She stopped and dismounted and laughed at him. He was wearing an open-necked shirt and an old pair of gardening trousers which he had borrowed.

'Where are your things?'

'In the saddle bag,' he replied.

'My saddle bag is full of food, and there's a basket, too.'

'Good. Is this the spot?'

'That's right.'

They pushed the bicycles clear of the road and hid them among some bushes and then, carrying the food, they walked along the path for perhaps half a mile until they came to a small clearing near the southern shore of the loch. It was screened from the road by trees and bushes, but even so they had quite a good view of the loch stretching eastwards, and of the hills all round. It was utterly peaceful and there was a small stream beside which they sat.

'That is it,' Fiona announced. 'Guaranteed free from interruption.'

'Perfect.'

He lay down on the thick springy turf and clasped his hands behind his head. Fiona lay on her stomach and chewed the end of a blade of grass.

'Is this what we do?' he asked. 'Stay here all day?'

'No, later on if you like we can follow the path a bit further. It goes quite a way up into the hills. I thought we could rest for a little, have a cup of coffee and relax before exploring.'

'A jolly good idea too.'

They sat and talked for about an hour, mostly about Oxford which Fiona had never visited. He had enjoyed his undergraduate days and was only too happy to discuss them. Later they set off along the path, climbing upwards towards the peaks which lay only a mile or two to the south, rising to almost three thousand feet. The exercise, the warm sun, and the scenery all contributed to a sense of well being. They had their first snack on a hillside high above Loch Eilt. Afterwards they had another when they got back to the clearing. Fiona was amazed when she realized suddenly that it was after four o'clock.

'Heavens, look at the time,' she exclaimed.

He glanced at his wrist watch and grinned at her. 'It's hours till bedtime.'

'Maybe, but I can't stay any longer. I've got to go home.'

'That's a pity. It's been a lovely day and I don't want to see it end,' he sighed.

'I hope it made a change, as I promised,' she said.

'Of course it did, Fiona. I haven't exjoyed myself so much for a very long time. I can't put it into words.'

'I've enjoyed it too.'

'Have you?' he asked. 'Wasn't there some talk about a special prize?'

'I'd forgotten,' she laughed. 'I'm afraid that was only a figure of speech.'

'Still, I have won it, haven't I?' he insisted.

She had got up and was dusting bits of grass from her skirt.

'Yes you have.'

He startled her by taking her in his arms and kissing her. The kiss went on and on until she pushed herself free.

'There's no need to smother me,' she said with a shaky little laugh.

'You did say a special prize, not an ordinary one.'

Fiona was aware of her heart thumping loudly. 'I think

you should remember that I'm married,' she said a little stiffly and awkwardly.

'I hadn't forgotten. On the other hand you should remember that I'm not married and that all's fair, even in war.'

She was embarrassed, and to hide it she answered, 'There, you've spoiled it. We weren't going to mention that word.'

'It's all over now. We're going home.'

'I know,' she said very quietly.

'When do I see you again?' he demanded.

'I don't know. I have other things to do, Norman. Some time soon.'

'Oh Fiona, you can do better than that.'

'Well . . . come round next week-end, on Sunday morning. Come to Castlemore but bring three or four other people with you. I'll tell Norma I invited you all yesterday and that it slipped my mind.'

'I want to see you alone,' he complained.

'We can't always have what we want, Norman, none of us. Anyway, it's better you don't.'

He was silent till they had collected their bicycles and were standing on the road again.

'Thank you, Fiona. Please do it again some time. I promise to behave.'

'All right, but not too soon. It would look bad and people might misunderstand.'

His face broke into a grin. 'As long as I have something definite to look forward to,' he told her. 'Lochailort is a little overpoweringly male, you know. Besides, there's another reason . . .'

He waved and cycled off. She set off in the opposite direction more slowly. Why had she done it, she wondered? It was risky and foolish, making dates with this rather handsome Army officer with the gift for saying the unexpected. Probably he was younger than herself – she must find out about that. What had he meant . . . 'Besides, there's another reason'? She thought she knew and she wondered why she didn't mind.

Norma saw the difference in Fiona and wondered at it. The subdued air had gone, the girl sparkled. She wondered about Norman Windsor, with whom Fiona had been just a little indiscreet on the day of the buffet lunch at Lochailort. She said nothing, partly because she did not wish to provoke a crisis, and partly because she might be wrong. She still found it difficult to believe that anyone married to Alasdair Beg could find consolation in other people. She watched Fiona and Lieutenant Norman Windsor on the next two occasions that he came to the house with other officers from Lochailort, but they were very circumspect.

That summer Deirdre came home from Miss Weir's for the last time, a very grown-up seventeen. She was due to go to Aberdeen University in September where she wanted to read history. She was tall, fair-haired, with blue-grey eyes and a full soft mouth. She was a very attractive young woman. She had passed her driving test during the Easter holidays and Norma decided to allow her to drive them home from the railway station.

Norma had gone to Fort William about two hours early and spent the time with Susan at Grunaglack. She found Susan quite upset, and not at all her usual snooty self.

'Is something wrong?' she asked in the direct way she used occasionally.

Susan bit her lip and nodded.

'I don't like talking about it, but it's a relief to be able to say something. Of course it mustn't go any further.'

'What mustn't?' Norma asked.

'The news. I've had a letter from Linda Bateman. I knew her in Paris and she's a great friend. We write to one another often.'

'What news?' Norma asked patiently.

'Sorry, I'm so upset I scarcely know what to say. It's about Maurice. He's having an affair in Washington.'

'Can you be sure?' Norma asked doubtfully. 'It might be pure gossip.'

'I can be sure if Linda says so. She says it's being whispered everywhere. Of course Maurice is discreet, but you can't hide that sort of thing for long.'

'In that case what are you going to do? Who is the woman?'

'I'm not going to do anything,' Susan flashed. 'Not a thing, and if he asks for a divorce I shall refuse it.'

'Very sensible. When he comes home he'll snap out of it.'

'Snap out of it, indeed! How horrible men are. I couldn't bear to touch him after this.'

Susan was a picture of outraged virtue. It was too bad of Maurice, Norma thought, although from what she had been able to piece together from conversations Maurice was sorely tried and had never wanted to go to Washington alone.

'Who is she?' Norma asked again.

'Oh, some secretary, would you believe it? Some cheap and nasty little working-class slut. Her name is Joanna Fairburn, Linda says.'

'Is she a secretary in the British Embassy?' Norma enquired, ignoring the somewhat slanted assessment of the girl's character.

'No, of course not. Maurice has more sense than to behave badly with one of the girls on his own staff. She works in the Pentagon, if you please.'

Norma wondered vaguely if Susan was blaming the President in some way.

'Of course it can do Maurice's career no good,' Susan went on waspishly. 'I'm sure the Ambassador knows about it. It's such a pity. Maurice is Head of Chancery you know, and a Counsellor – he'll be due for an embassy when he leaves Washington. He won't get it, of course.'

'Really?' Norma asked, surprised.

'Of course not. An ambassador is supposed to be a gentleman, after all.'

Norma wondered whether, in the world of men inhabited by Lord Maurice Blood, his little affair with a secretary would really ruin his career – always assuming that he continued to be discreet. After all his wife had refused to accompany him abroad. What was he supposed to do?

'I'm sorry, Susan,' she said, gathering her wandering thoughts. She really was sorry too. She did not like to see unhappiness in the family, and towards Gordon and Susan she had a special feeling because she felt that they had had such an unsatisfactory father in the much-married Charles. 'I'm sure it will pass.'

'It will have to. I've written to him of course.'

'Without being positive?' Norma asked horrified. 'I hope you haven't said anything unfair.'

'I've told him he's to stop seeing the girl at once, otherwise I shall write to the Ambassador and ask for him to be sent home. That will stop him. You've no idea how stuffy Maurice is about the Foreign Office. The threat of a letter will stop him.'

Norma gaped. It would stop him all right, but it would drive him further away from Susan. To write to the Ambassador complaining about her husband's conduct was an act of such disloyalty that Norma could hardly believe it. It might very easily terminate his career. Even if it didn't, it would be affected for ever afterwards.

'I hope it turns out all right,' she said feebly.

'It will. I reminded him about the boys. They wouldn't like to know the truth about their aristocratic father.'

'You threatened him with the children?' Norma wondered.

'Sort of.' Susan gave a wintry smile. 'I *hinted* would be a better way of putting it. Maurice Blood had better learn that he can't play fast and loose with me.'

No doubt he would learn, poor man, Norma thought. What a horrible prig Susan could be. There would be trouble at Grunaglack, that much was obvious.

'I'm visiting his family at the end of the year,' Susan went on. 'Maurice's sister, Lady Alys, has asked us to the Cotswolds for Christmas. It will make a change for Vernon and Philip.'

'Yes of course. Where does she live? I know very little about Maurice's family.'

'She lives just outside Cirencester with her husband, Jasper Williams. He has a riding school there and breeds horses. There's a little bit of land too, a small farm. I shall be going as soon as the boys' Christmas holidays begin, in mid-December, and staying for about a month. Maurice knows that, of course. He won't want me to have anything unsavoury to report to his sister, I'm sure.'

They had tea together, and Susan changed the conversation and talked about Deirdre who was due at lunchtime.

'It's very good of you, looking after her, you know.'

'She's an extremely fine girl. I'm terribly proud of her,' Norma said complacently.

'Perhaps, but even so . . . there's her background.'

'It's a perfectly good background. Her mother wasn't exactly upper class, but the Mathiesons were a very nice family. I still write to old Mrs Mathieson in Perth.'

'I was thinking of Bobbie – twice in prison, and being unmarried. What chance does the girl have of making a suitable marriage with such a handicap?'

'Every chance,' Norma said, flushing a little. 'I hope you don't discuss Deirdre or her parents with other people, Susan.'

'No of course not.'

'Some things are private, matters for the family only. I wouldn't like to learn that other people were bandying them about.'

'I'm sure I don't know what gives you the idea that

I'd talk about Bobbie to anyone,' Susan retorted stiffly. 'I'm only too glad to pretend he never existed.'

'Susan, you're a fool,' Norma said bluntly, losing her patience. 'I'm very fond of you and I'm very sorry for you, because your father was an even bigger fool, but I have no illusions about you. If Maurice leaves you for another woman it will be your own fault entirely. That's your business, but I warn you that you're going about it all the wrong way. Try a little understanding and sympathy. It works wonders as often as not. Anyway, as I said, that's your own affair, but Deirdre is my affair. Bobbie was an infinitely finer man than your father. I'm sorry, but it's the truth.'

'That gaol bird,' the outraged Susan gasped, scarlet with rage.

'Yes, he was in prison twice, and he overcame it. Just before he died he was named as a member of a Commission on Scottish Prison Reform. It was a great honour. Those who knew Bobbie admired him – and they all knew he had been in prison. As for his not being married, Alison was married to an absolutely drunken beast who deliberately refused to divorce her, just to make life miserable for her and for Bobbie. I'm sorry Susan, but they overcame great handicaps and difficulties and they overcame them splendidly. Charles was an amiable clown, a child in the hands of women, and a gambler who lost all his money. If it is of any interest to you, I liked Charles just as I liked all Dair's brothers, but that doesn't mean that I'm blind about their various virtues and faults.'

'Well, really!' Susan gaped.

'It's time someone told you, Susan. You're becoming an insufferable, overbearing woman. We all love you and we'd like to see you snap out of it.'

'Insulting me in my own home,' Susan gasped. 'You've no business to speak to me like that.'

'Your mother's dead. Who else is there?'

There was a very awkward silence during which Norma drank her tea with every outward appearance of calmness, although in truth her heart was beating painfully. She had always avoided scenes, but this one had been brewing ever since Susan had come home. It was for Susan's own sake.

'How is Alasdair?' Susan asked in a subdued voice, averting her eyes.

'Very well. He says he likes the desert. The 1st Grampians have just arrived out there and the two battalions have met at some place with a name I can neither pronounce nor spell. Alasdair was full of the news.'

'I'm glad he's well.'

'I don't think they'll kill Alasdair the way they killed his father,' Norma said quietly. 'I have a feeling he'll come home from the war. It's just a feeling.'

'I hope you're right.'

Norma nodded. She did have this feeling about Alasdair, but she also had a nagging foreboding of tragedy which puzzled her. She did not like to dwell too much on such things. She was growing old and fanciful, she thought.

She left a rather shattered Susan behind her and drove the car through the town to the railway station. Fiona had not accompanied her, mainly because Fiona could not stand Susan and preferred to avoid her, and when she'd heard that Norma intended to visit Grunaglack she had begged off. Norma had not pressed the point. She knew from long experience that it was better to let such situations sort themselves out in their own good time.

When the train arrived she spotted Deirdre almost at once, in her school uniform of grey worsted suit, white blouse, and maroon tie and hat. Well, she wouldn't be wearing that again, Norma thought as she advanced on the girl, arms outstretched.

'Hullo, Aunt Norma.' Deirdre hugged her. 'You look younger than ever.'

'Oh rubbish. You're looking prettier than ever.'

'You see, we approve of one another. Where's Fiona?'

'At home. She sent her apologies. I've been at Gruna-glack and Fiona didn't want to come along.'

'I see. Let's get my trunk.'

They collected her trunk and suitcase, and a porter put them in the back of the car.

'You drive,' Norma said, and with a delighted smile Deirdre slid behind the wheel and started up.

'That's the end of your schooldays,' Norma said, settling more comfortably beside her. 'You're a woman now.'

'I know. I like it. I did wish I could have a car of my own.'

'The war can't last for ever,' Norma assured her.

They had agreed that with petrol rationing it was hardly worth buying a car for Deirdre, especially as she did not actually need one. She was to get a car either when she was twenty-one or when the war ended, which-ever was first. Meantime she drove the family car on her holidays with all the enthusiasm of someone to whom driving was still a novelty. Norma would be glad to have a chauffeur again one day.

When they arrived back at Castlemore, Fiona came out to the car and embraced her husband's young cousin. Ipla helped them with the trunk, and then they had lunch before Fiona and Deirdre went upstairs together to un-pack Deirdre's trunk and sort out all the things which could be given away.

The following morning the mail included a rare letter to Norma from May in Hereford. Norma read it twice and then handed it to Fiona. The letter was all about someone called Edward Gentle whom May had met in Hereford where he was stationed with the Royal Air Force. He was eighteen months older than May and was a regular R.A.F. officer but not a flier, as Boy Loring had been. Gentle had gone to university and then into the

R.A.F. where he was an equipment officer. He was already a Wing Commander, which Norma supposed was quite good for someone on the ground staff who was only thirty.

The difficulty, as May wrote, was that Edward Gentle had a wife already, although he had separated from her and had not seen her for over two years. He would see about a divorce. Meantime, divorce or no divorce, they were in love and he stayed with her at the cottage in Weobley as often as he could. She was very happy.

Fiona handed back the letter.

'I hope it works out for them. May deserves a little luck,' she said.

'It doesn't say much about his wife,' Norma mused. 'I wonder what she thinks of it all. May forgets sometimes that other people have their own view of life. A divorce might not be so easily arranged.'

'We must just hope, mustn't we?' Fiona asked.

'I suppose so.'

'You don't sound enthusiastic.'

'I'm old fashioned,' Norma replied. 'I don't mean I think May's a scarlet woman or anything so dramatic, but I just wish she could have picked on someone who was free to marry her. I've never learned to feel comfortable about affairs involving married men or women.'

Fiona wondered fleetingly if that was a dig at herself. She tried hard not to reveal her deep interest in Norman Windsor, but it was difficult. She had a horrible suspicion that she was completely transparent, that Norma could see through her.

'If she loves Wing Commander Gentle, that's all there is to it,' Fiona said simply.

Norma nodded, rather miserable. No good came of such liaisons, she was sure of it.

7

They had been hoarding petrol and during the summer
they went out in the car several times, to Mallaig, down
to Oban, and across country to Inverness and to Aberdeen. One of the officers at Lochailort had done something to the car engine so that it got slightly more miles to
the gallon. It was the first time anyone at Castlemore had
ever troubled about anything so trivial as how many miles
a car did to a gallon of petrol, except Alasdair Beg who
liked sports cars and thought that the fewer miles he got
to the gallon the better his car.

By now they knew that Lochailort was a commando
training school and that all the soldiers there were commandos. This lent them a certain glamour, especially in
Deirdre's young eyes. There were several picnics locally
and more than one young commando officer far from
home looked at Deirdre with calculating eyes. Fiona
stood guard over her young cousin like a watchful hen
protecting her brood. One evening at the height of summer four of the officers on the staff came over for dinner.
Leona had come up from Ardclune for the night, leaving
Eve and Mary in the charge of Finvola. There were eight
of them to dinner, and it was quite a gay party. Norman
Windsor managed to persuade Fiona to walk in the garden with him and they ended up in the summer house.

'I thought I'd never get you alone again,' he laughed,
taking her in his arms and kissing her.

'Don't do that here, Norman. Someone might see.'

'All right. I'm sorry. It that all you're worried about –
that someone might see?'

She coloured prettily. 'I'd rather not talk about it.'

'I rather would. Anyway, when are we having a picnic
again? You said we could.'

'It's too risky.'

'Damn the risk. Listen Fiona, I love you. You must know that.'

'You're being silly, Norman,' she said desperately. 'I'm married. I'm even older than you are.'

'Only two years, and what does that matter anyway? You mustn't think in conventional clichés, Fiona.'

'I'm thinking of my husband who's out in North Africa fighting. I'm not going to do anything to hurt him.'

He was silent for a few moments. 'At least we can have a picnic, can't we?' he asked at last. 'I'm sorry I told you how I feel about you. It was impertinent, but you must realize, Fiona, that I find life at Lochailort frustrating with all those fire-eating warmongers. I hate the war. It's ugly and stupid and wasteful. You're like an oasis in a desert of male insanity.'

'I'm not sure that that's flattering,' she laughed.

'I'm not in the mood for pretty speeches. I mean it Fiona – my meetings with you are things I treasure. We both feel the same way about things.'

'I'm not so sure that we do,' she temporized.

'We do,' he affirmed. 'We're rebels against all the materialistic things that lead to wars – flag-waving, nationalism, pursuit of wealth, grinding other people down – these are the things that produce the climate in which wars flourish. You know it and I know it. How the hell did you ever come to marry a regular soldier?'

'I was in love with him. He's a very fine man. He believes in things like duty and self-sacrifice, and honour isn't just a word to him.'

'I'm not running him down,' Norman said desperately. 'It's just that I can see behind the façade which probably he accepts at face value – and you can see behind it too. I want to talk to you about beauty and peace. Do I sound stupid?'

'No.' She shook her head and smiled. 'You're not stupid at all. I like talking to you. I tell you what, get someone else and we'll make up a foursome quite openly. I'll bring Deirdre along.'

'I can think of several youngsters who'd be delighted to go on a picnic with that particular young lady. She's the talk of the Mess. She's our pin-up girl – not mine of course, but you'd be surprised how many of them talk about her.'

'Is that so? She's only seventeen.'

'That makes her a woman. Anyway, I'll find someone. When?'

'Next week-end?'

'Yes, that's okay. Sunday morning?'

'That's right. Ten o'clock. Let's go to Glenfinnan shall we? I've got a little petrol to spare.'

'I'll wangle a jeep. You leave it to me.'

'I thought you couldn't do that? Go on a picnic to Glenfinnan in Army transport?' she asked.

'I'm becoming as crafty as the worst of them,' Norman chuckled. 'I'll fix it.'

'Good. Now we must go back inside.'

'If you say so.'

He stood aside and let her lead the way. He wanted to kiss her again but he knew instinctively that it would be a mistake. She was fighting her own battle with herself, and her conscience was giving her a lot of trouble. He could do nothing to influence her without damaging his own case.

When Fiona mentioned the picnic to Norma, Norma sighed.

'Fiona, does Norman Windsor mean anything to you? You see him quite often, don't you?'

'Not too often,' she protested. 'I've met him several times and I met him at that buffet lunch they gave over at Lochailort, that's all.'

'I've noticed you and he go off together to talk privately. I wondered.'

'Wondered what?' Fiona asked stiffly and Norma

knew she had bungled it. She wished she had kept silent.

'You're young and Alasdair has been away for a long time and may be away for a long time to come. It would be natural if you looked for . . . pleasant company.'

'I suppose I do,' Fiona said lightly. 'I hadn't thought about it much. I like Norman Windsor. He's a little bit less hearty than some of the others, less bloodthirsty.'

'He seems very nice, but do be careful won't you? Young men, in war-time, don't always behave as they would normally.'

'Thanks.' Fiona laughed again. 'I think I can defend my honour.'

Norma was glad to let it rest there, and determined to mind her own business in future. The picnic was a model of propriety for Fiona and Deirdre were never out of one another's sight. Even so a breathless young Lieutenant found an opportunity to make a clumsy proposal which was Deidre's first, and Fiona and Norman were able to speak together privately.

'They won't keep me here for ever, you know,' Norman said. 'One day they'll say I've had enough time playing at being an instructor and they'll post me to one of the commandos. I'll be sent away and I may not be able to come back for a long time.'

'I know,' Fiona admitted glumly.

'I've been lucky to stay here so long, when we had so many losses at St Nazaire. I don't want to go away, Fiona.'

'I don't want you to go,' she agreed in a low voice.

'Can't you leave your husband? You know I love you. Surely you feel something for me.'

'I can't leave Alasdair. You don't know what you're asking me to do.'

She was thinking of Castlemore, of Norma, of Deidre – in truth it was a great deal more than just leaving Alasdair, and in any case how *could* she leave him in the lurch while he was fighting in the Western Desert?

'You do love me, don't you?' he urged.

'You mustn't ask me that.'

'Why not, it's true isn't it? Isn't it, Fiona?' He spoke in a quiet but urgent voice.

After a moment she nodded. 'It's madness, but I do. Listen Norman, I shan't walk out on my husband, not when he's overseas like this.'

'When he comes home then?'

'We'll see.'

'Don't play games with me, please. I can stand not being able to touch you, or kiss you, even not seeing you very often, as long as I know that one day it will end. Will you marry me when you're free?'

'I may not *be* free.'

'I'll make a deal with you,' he whispered. 'You tell him after the war, just as soon as the war's over. Meantime I'll write to you, and you'll write to me, we'll meet when we can, and we'll be very very discreet. Is that a bargain?'

'All right,' she said, suddenly giving in.

'You do love me.'

'Yes, you know I do,' she answered. 'God forgive me.'

'That's a cheerful thing to say,' he replied gaily. 'Thank you Fiona. Thank you for giving me something to live for.'

'This is folly,' she said sadly. 'There's a war on. Alasdair is an infantry officer and you're a commando. Who are we to talk about living? I may end up with neither of you.'

'That would be your tragedy,' he agreed mildly. 'I hope it never comes to pass.'

Somehow after that confession of her feelings, Fiona felt more cheerful. One could endure anything, as Norman had said, as long as one believed that at the end it would all come right.

On the 19th of August the Dieppe raid took place and

although the Canadians bore the brunt of the losses, Fiona's heart beat a little faster when she heard the official news releases. They might post Norman away to a fighting unit. He had just beem promoted Captain. How much time did he have in the safety and seclusion of the Scottish Highlands?

The summer ended in a flurry of packing and seeing Deirdre off to Aberdeen. Afterwards the house seemed empty again as it always did when Deirdre went away. Pal Al and Frances Mary were at school all day in the local village school to which they cycled. Fiona considered leaving Castlemore and going south to take up war work of some sort but, as always, she thought of the children and of Castlemore itself. She dismissed the idea. There were plenty of other women without her. Yet there was a strain in waiting, waiting for something to happen. What?

In November came more news of Alasdair's successes. He had been awarded the Distinguished Service Order, promoted to Lieutenant-Colonel and given his own beloved 1st battalion to command. The long letter in which he told Fiona the news was literally bubbling over with pride and joy. Now he was really following in his father's footsteps. He never talked about the end of the war, or about coming home. He seemed to be perfectly happy with things as they were.

Pal Al, of course, reacted in a very positive way to the news. He was enormously proud of his father and thought that the war was something expressly designed to give good soldiers an opportunity to show what they could do. He knew all about his grandfather who had been killed in battle in 1917 and who was a hero; and now his own father, whom he had always worshipped, was a Colonel and had more medals.

'Will there be a war when I grow up?' he asked Norma just after Alasdair's letter arrived. 'I mean, it won't be much fun being in the Army if there's no war, Gran, will it?' Usually he talked to Norma rather than to Fiona, for Fiona had depressing views on life, saying that war was silly and that she hoped this one would end soon and that there would never be a war again. Pal Al could not conceive a world in which there would be no wars. He was an avid reader of history, which, to his joy, he had discovered at school was all about kings and wars. He liked kings and wars. If he were a king he'd start lots of wars of his own, jolly good ones too in which he'd win all the medals.

For a split second Norma was carried back in time to that day early in 1918 when Captain Wallace had come home from France bringing Dair's sword and one or two other things. Alasdair Beg had pleaded for the sword, she remembered. He had wanted to hang it on the wall of his bedroom, as he had done in fact. She remembered how upset she had been at first, how bitter about the Army which had taken Dair from her. What was it that had happened? Alasdair Beg had said that he was going to be a Colonel too, and that he was going to join his father's regiment and win the next war. She had told him angrily that there would be no war.

'What shall I do then?' he had asked dejectedly, and then more defiantly he had waved the sword and shouted, 'There *will* be a war. I know there will.'

How true it had all turned out to be. There was a war, he was a Colonel, commanding the 1st Grampians just as he had always wanted. Would history repeat itself yet again, she asked herself?

'Gran?' Pal Al asked anxiously. 'Is something wrong?'

'No, darling. I was thinking of your father. You're so like him.'

'I want to be like him. I want to join the Grampians and be a hero too. Wouldn't it be great if I could be a Colonel like my father?'

'Yes,' Norma said without conviction.

'I wonder if I could get the V.C.,' Pal Al mused. He

was quite an authority on medals, badges of rank and other technical aspects of the Army.

'It will be better if your father comes home safely.'

'Oh yes,' Pal Al agreed. 'I wonder if he'll be promoted again next year.'

Norma watched him as he ran upstairs, a sturdy little kilted figure. She wondered how Fiona would react if Pal Al decided he wanted to go into the Army. It was the obvious career for him and Alasdair Beg almost certainly planned it that way, yet Norma doubted if Fiona would submit without protest. Fiona had never learned to accept the inevitable, not where the Army was concerned.

She sat there, hands folded quietly in her lap, looking out of the window. The war had made a mess of all their lives. May was in love with a married R.A.F. officer, herself a widow at thirty. Susan and Leona were separated from their husbands and Susan's marriage was threatened by unhappiness, if not by something worse. What of Fiona? She wished she understood Fiona better, but there was still a barrier between them, not an obvious one perhaps, but it was there.

It would be all right when Alasdair came home.

On the 6th of March 1943, at a place called Medenine in North Africa, Alasdair Robert MacInnes won the Victoria Cross. Rommel, who had broken through the Kasserine Pass, turned on the Eighth Army and was repulsed. Some of the repulsing was done by the 1st Grampians, who were decimated in the process. Alasdair was not killed, but he was shipped home in the summer, a broken man. He had been shot in sundry places and these numerous wounds had healed quickly and fairly satisfactorily. Unfortunately he had also been badly shot in the shoulder and his right arm had had to be amputated as a result of an infection.

When at last he arrived back at Castlemore they were dismayed by the sight of him. It was not merely the empty right sleeve, for which they had been prepared, but he limped also and his face was badly disfigured and scarred.

A shrapnel wound in the mouth had given it a funny downward twist. He was the handsome soldier no more, but a dispirited wreck of a man.

When she met him at the station Fiona had turned as white as a sheet, but she managed to control her emotions, kissed him affectionately, fussed over him, and spoke in a voice which hid the turmoil of her thoughts. Norma and the children had stayed at home at Fiona's request. She wanted to meet her husband alone. Now she wondered what they'd say.

'How do you feel?' she asked as she drove rather slowly back along the road towards Castlemore.

'Not too bright. My arm hurts a lot – the arm they cut off. It's quite true what they say about an amputated limb aching. There's also some shrapnel in my spine which they've left inside and that jabs at me. I'm afraid I look a wreck, darling.'

'Never mind, you're home and that's all that matters.'

'Yes, home.' He spoke with infinite sadness. 'Home for ever, a crock. I'm out of the Army now, just when I had everything I wanted – the command of the battalion, a bright future . . . oh I can't tell you. Now I'm a has-been.'

'They've given you the V.C. darling. You're part of the history of the regiment. You're even part of the history of the country. Your name will be in all sorts of books.'

'That's right, history at thirty-three. Bloody funny.'

'Poor Alasdair. It isn't as bad as you think. When do you get an artificial limb?'

'I don't want one. I refused it.'

'You did what?'

He shrugged. 'I said no. I can't stand the sight of them. I'm learning to use my left hand for everything. I can dress myself and even manage my shoes, although I never did like shoelaces. I shall have some shoes designed, like evening brogues only without the buckle on the toe – or like slippers, perhaps. Laces are out of date, it's time we got rid of them.'

'You mean you're not going to have a right arm at all?'

'That's what I've been telling you. Who wants to take their arm off at night and put it on again in the morning? It's grotesque. As for a funny pincer-like contraption for a hand . . . I ask you!'

'You could have a dummy, like the real thing.'

'What good's that if you can't use it? I don't need a false arm. I'm all right.'

He spoke stubbornly, and she abandoned the topic. He must be shocked still. He would come round in the end.

'Do you sleep all right?' she asked.

'Oh yes, usually. I get funny sorts of dizzy spells and I see colours that aren't there. Sometimes I don't see colours at all – the world goes sort of black and white. I've seen the doctors but they say it's just strain and that it will go away. I hope so. It's a damned nuisance.'

'You don't have to go away again soon?' she asked.

'No. The doctors want to see me in Edinburgh in about a month's time, just for a routine check up. That's all.'

'Pal Al was so proud of your V.C.'

'I'm glad. It isn't much to have to show for a right arm, is it? I suppose I have to go on to an investiture some time. They'll be letting me know.'

'Yes of course.'

'I'll take you and young Al, if that's all right.'

'We are looking forward to it, darling.'

'It's nice to see the old place again after so long. I thought so often about coming back to you, but I never imagined it would be like this.'

'You never said anything in letters.'

'Well, one doesn't want to dwell on things like coming home when one's overseas.'

'I got the impression that you liked the desert.'

'I did, I loved it, and we had a grand bunch of chaps

I wouldn't have missed it for anything. It's just hard luck we got in Rommel's way as we did. Everything had been going so well for me too. Let's not talk about it, darling. Give me all the news. I must catch up.'

They were standing on the top of the stone steps, under the portico, when the car drove up – Norma, Deirdre, Pal Al and little Frances Mary. His V.C. had been announced about a month after his wounds and they were tremendously proud of him. When the door opened and he stepped out, a little bent, his face disfigured, his empty sleeve pinned to his right breast, and he limped awkwardly towards them, Pal Al let out a cry of anguish.

'No!' he screamed. 'No, no, *no*.'

Instead of running towards his father he turned his back and fled into the house. Norma was completely taken aback. She also was hit hard by her son's appearance, but Al had been so filled with hero worship since the V.C. had been announced that he had not seemed at all upset to learn that his father had lost an arm. His only remark had been that Nelson had lost an arm and an eye, which Norma had thought rather callous.

He's only eight, she thought sadly as she watched Alasdair. Frances Mary's hand crept into hers and she squeezed it gently. Beside her Deirdre stood, frozen faced.

'Hullo,' Alasdair said, trying to be bright. 'Poor little Al. I'm afraid he's upset.'

'Darling,' Norma said, her voice breaking, and she embraced him carefully.

'Mama.'

'Come inside.'

They were standing just inside the door, Mrs Mac-Donald, Euphemia and Ipla, all that was left of the servants. They caught their breath but their welcome was genuine enough. Alasdair beamed at them, his eyes bright. Then they took him into the sitting room and Fiona poured him a drink.

Norma slipped away and found Pal Al in his bedroom. He lay on his bed, his face buried in the bedspread, his shoulders heaving. She sat beside him and put an arm on his shoulder.

'Al, you must come down and see your father.'

'I don't want to,' the boy sobbed, broken-hearted. 'I can't.'

'Al, your father is a hero. He was wounded fighting for his country.'

'You said he'd had his arm cut off. You didn't say he'd look so ... so ... he frightens me.'

'Poor child. Do you think he likes it? Frances Mary didn't run away, did she?'

There was a silence and eventually he sat up and turned a tear-stained face to her.

'I thought war was fun,' he said brokenly. 'It isn't. I hate the Army.'

'Well, my dear, that's no reason to run away from your father. You've hurt him, Al, and he's been hurt enough already.'

'I'm sorry.'

'Shall we go down?'

'Yes, Gran.'

He took her hand and went downstairs with her. He found it difficult to look his father in the eye, but Alasdair made it easy for him, his manner relaxed and jovial.

'Hullo, young man. You've grown tall while I've been away. How's school?'

'All right thanks.'

'You look fine. You all look fine. It's quite like old times, all being together, isn't it?'

'Yes,' Pal Al agreed in a very subdued voice.

It was not at all like old times, as they soon realized. For one thing, it was clear that something was wrong with Alasdair. His dizzy spells were fairly frequent and he felt ill quite often; also he was increasingly bad tempered, sometimes unreasonably so. He seemed to find fault with everything and he hated being interrupted when he was 'thinking', which was fairly often. Even Norma, who had always been prepared for this eventuality, found it difficult to live with the son who seemed to be crippled mentally as well as physically.

After one particularly awkward breakfast, Pal Al surprised Fiona. He came to her in her room and stood awkwardly.

'Mummy.'

'Yes, darling?'

'Will I *have* to go into the Army?'

'Not if you don't want to, darling.'

'What could I do instead?'

'I don't know. You're much too young to worry about that. We must wait till you're older. You could go to university, like Deirdre.'

'I think I'd like that, but I don't want to learn any more history.'

'I see.' Fiona averted her head. 'There are other things. Just be patient, darling.'

'Daddy said last night that I can have his sword if I want, the one that belonged to Grandfather.'

'Did he? Are you pleased?'

'Not specially, but I said all right.'

'I think that was the correct thing to say. Al, Daddy isn't well yet. He's still ill and you must be patient.'

'I know. I wish the holidays were over. I want to go back to school.'

Fiona had her own problems. Norman Windsor had telephoned when Alasdair's V.C. had been announced.

'You can leave him now,' he said crisply. 'He's got the V.C. What more does he want?'

'Norman, he's lost an arm.'

'I'm very sorry for him, but it's not the end of the world. Lots of people are much worse off than that. Look here, darling, he's coming home covered in glory. Now's the time to tell him, when he has other things to console him.'

'Be patient,' was all she would say.

Now she telephoned him in the Mess one evening.

'Norman, can you possibly meet me?'

'Yes, if you want. When and where?'

'It's very awkward. You managed to get hold of a jeep once. Could you do it again one night?'

'At night? I think so. What is it?'

'Listen, you know our summer house?'

'Of course I do.'

'Can you drive over, hide the jeep off the road somewhere, and meet me in the summer house at midnight?'

'Tonight you mean?'

'Any night.'

'Tonight then. I think I can fiddle it all right. If not I'll come on a bicycle anyway, so don't worry.'

'All right Norman. I'll see you at midnight.'

They were in the habit of going to bed shortly after ten-thirty, so that when she crept downstairs at a quarter to twelve the whole house was still and silent. She undid the glass-fronted door in the hall and tiptoed out. The wooden outer doors were never closed in summer. She went to the summer house and waited. Upstairs Norma, who was sitting at her window, unable to sleep, watched and wondered.

At two minutes to twelve Norman arrived at the summer house. He took her in his arms and she let him kiss her. She clung to him desperately.

'Is something wrong?' he asked at last.

'Yes, terribly wrong.'

'What?' He felt afraid.

'Norman, I can't leave him. I can't possibly.'

'Damn, why not?'

'He's a wreck. You need to see him to realize it. He's shattered physically and mentally. It isn't just an arm, believe me, it's far worse. He's ill, he looks awful – he got shrapnel in the face – his nerves are absolutely raw. He's only a shadow of the man who went away.'

Norman was silent. He could fight most things but he could not fight a wounded hero, not one who was in the condition Fiona described.

'How long do we have to wait now?' he asked.

'I don't know.' She wrung her hands unconsciously. 'I can't see the end of it at all.'

'Are you trying to say it's all over between us?'

She hesitated and then nodded. 'I think so.'

'No!'

'You ought to see him. I tell you what, I'll telephone in the morning and ask a few of you over to lunch on Saturday. You'll see for yourself. You can write to me afterwards and say what you think.'

'Oh that's great.'

'What else can I do except ask you to form your own impression? Do you think I like this?'

'I'm sorry. I'm not usually prone to self-pity. All right, I'll see him on Saturday and I'll write to you. It's unfair that both our lives should be spoiled because of one man.'

'Perhaps it is. Is life meant to be fair anyway? I've never been sure of an answer to that.'

'Kiss me before I go,' he said.

She did so, hugging him to her desperately, their lips fused in a passion that shook them both, a passion which fed on itself and which found no release. At last he tore himself away and left her. Norma, still sitting at the window, thought that his shoulders seemed bowed. What had been going on, she wondered? She waited for another fifteen minutes till Fiona returned to the house, and this time it was a different Fiona, one who shuffled instead of walked, one who even in the pale indistinct light of the moon seemed older than the girl who had gone out just before midnight.

Norma was not entirely surprised when Fiona said she had invited half a dozen officers from Lochailort for lunch on Saturday. Despite rationing they could usually put on a decent meal, for there was a fair supply of fish and rabbits as well as their own poultry which Norma kept now. Norma rarely had a spare moment and time never hung heavily on her hands. She had the gift of keeping herself both occupied and interested. She and Deirdre worked in the garden together that summer and they were as brown as berries. Fiona spent long hours sitting with Alasdair, just keeping him company.

They were the usual gay high-spirited bunch of officers, except for Norman who was much quieter than usual. Of course they were all interested to meet the local hero, the Highlander who had won the Victoria Cross. It was obvious that they were embarrassed when they saw him, even though it was one of his better days. He wore a kilt and looked well in it, and his limp was less pronounced. The doctors said it would disappear in time except perhaps for twinges in the winter. There was talk about surgery to try to improve his appearance, but Alasdair did not seem very interested in this. In fact he was not very interested in anything, but the company of the commandos cheered him up a lot.

Norman was sitting beside Deirdre, toying with his food.

'How was your first year at university?' he asked.

'I liked it. I like Aberdeen, you know, and I've made a lot of interesting friends.'

'It's a bit more lively than this, I daresay.'

'Yes it is,' she laughed, 'but not nearly so beautiful. If Castlemore were mine I'd never go away.'

'What are you going to do when you get your degree?'

'Teach. I want to do a course and teach at an infant school. I like children, you see.'

'Infant school? Isn't that a waste of a degree?'

'I don't see why. You don't *need* one, but I don't think it's a waste. You've got a degree, haven't you?'

'True.'

'You don't use it in your work do you?'

'As a journalist? No, I don't suppose it's made much difference and certainly it won't after the war.'

'You see,' she laughed.

'All right, you've made your cunning point. I accept it. What's Fiona's husband going to do now, do you know?'

Deirdre's face clouded. 'Poor Alasdair. All he ever cared about was the Army. He was brought up for it, and he did succeed in realizing his ambitions, or one of them, for just a little while. He commanded the 1st battalion, like his father before him. I expect he'd have wanted to be a General, like General Charles.'

'Who's he?'

'Our great-grandfather. The man who bought this house in 1853.'

'I'm suitably impressed. Nevertheless, it leaves the question unanswered. What now?'

'Who can say? Fiona has a real burden to bear. He's so grouchy and miserable, and he gets these funny spells.'

'What do the doctors say?'

'Rest. Of course he's completely finished in the Army. Do you know he actually applied to stay on, in any capacity?'

'He's a demon for punishment,' Norman grunted.

'They turned him down. It isn't only his arm. You can see for yourself, and this is one of his very good days. The children have never really got used to him, and young Pal Al won't even talk about the Army any more, which must hurt Alasdair deeply, and Fiona's been like a ghost ever since he came home.'

'Perhaps she could get away for a bit?' he suggested.

'And leave him? She couldn't do that. It would be too heartless. He clings to her. It's funny, because I'd have thought he'd turn to his mother. Norma understands about the Army much better than Fiona does. Norma's been through all this herself.'

'I've heard the story.'

'Fiona's rather sceptical about all this death and glory business, yet it's to her that he turns. He's pathetically dependant on her. I don't mean he can't dress himself or anything, but even the most minor decision is referred to her. He always loved her, you see.'

She laughed self-consciously. 'That's an odd thing to say about someone's husband, isn't it? I mean, it was something special and now he feels helpless and hopeless. I think he feels he's failed in some way by being so badly knocked about.'

'Can't they do anything about him?'

'There's this new thing, what do they call it? Plastic surgery? They could improve his face a lot and he could get an artificial arm, but he's not at all interested. In fact he hates the idea of an artificial arm, and says his face doesn't matter. He may change later.'

'It's hard on Fiona, isn't it?' he asked, keeping his voice carefully controlled.

'Very. She's capable of so much fun, although it doesn't always show, and now she's bogged down with a life that is no fun for her at all. I suppose that's one of the risks of getting married.'

He nodded. He had been watching Alasdair during the conversation. He kept turning to Fiona for confirmation of all he said. It was true, he was dependent on her. It was a cruel business, and if he forced matters with Fiona he himself would only add to that cruelty.

He hadn't been hungry when he arrived. Now he lost his appetite altogether.

'Is something wrong?' Deirdre asked, noticing.

'No, just off my feed,' he joked. 'It must be love.'

8

Fiona re-read the letter with a heavy heart.

'Darling,' it read,

'You've made your point. As matters stand there is nothing for me to do but to bow and to withdraw as gracefully as I can. Obviously I can't go on like this, seeing you from time to time, never able to say the things I want, never able to hold you in my arms. It isn't fair to either of us. I have applied for a posting away from here, and I rather think I'll get it soon. I've had a good run as an instructor.

'It will be better if I don't write except to answer your letters. I don't want to make a nuisance of myself. I shall never know just how things are with you, whether a letter from me might make things worse, so you must take the initiative. You do see that, don't you?

'I have an address through which I can always be contacted. It is my bank in Oxford, the District Bank in High Street. A letter to me care of the bank will always reach me. Alternatively you can write to me care of my parents at Meadowbank, Market Drayton, Salop, but the bank is a safer bet because I'm rarely out of touch with my bank manager. He's far too useful to me.

'I know that mine is the easier path. I can go away, bury myself in new interests, go to new places, while you have to stay at Castlemore chained to your own sorrow. Don't think I shall love you any the less because I have the easier way, or that I shall not know what you are going through.

'I shan't see you again unless you send for me, nor

shall I write except to reply to you. I pray that this is not the end. After all we are both young, aren't we? Please don't forget me and please, if ever you want or need me, let me know. I do love you, and that is really all I need to say, isn't it?'

She made a note of both addresses in the back of her small crocodile-bound address book before shredding the letter. What he was doing was right. There was no future for them as things stood and there was no point in torturing themselves. Better a clean break, but how nice to know that he would always be there in the background, just in case.

Meantime Norma had unwillingly become involved in the affairs of Lord and Lady Maurice Blood. She had received a letter from Maurice in Washington. In it he told her quite bluntly that Susan wanted to divorce him. He had no intention of agreeing and he wondered if Norma could talk to Susan. He hoped Norma would forgive him for writing, but it was difficult when he was thousands of miles away and Susan was living virtually alone. 'You are, after all, the matriarch of the family,' he had written. 'Try to persuade Susan that everything will look different after the war. For the boys' sake I cannot countenance divorce. Perhaps I behaved foolishly but she has no grounds now for complaint.'

Norma had hesitated at first. She did not want to become involved in Susan's affairs and was astonished at Maurice writing to her as he had done. It was totally out of character and he must be very disturbed indeed. More than this, she was intrigued despite herself. Last time she had talked to Susan about Maurice, Susan had been threatening Maurice with all sorts of dire consequences unless he stopped seeing some secretary in Washington, but divorce had not been mentioned. Now it seemed that she did want a divorce. One had to admit that Susan had a gift for surprising them. In the end she invited Susan to Castlemore, suggesting that she come early for a talk. After all, she thought to herself, Susan had been hoarding petrol and could make the journey more easily than she could.

Susan was a fine-looking woman, Norma conceded, as the very well-dressed Lady Maurice walked beside her to the drawing room where they could be certain of being alone. Clothes rationing never seemed to worry Susan and Norma had a feeling that it would not be wise to enquire too closely into Susan's affairs. She was not the person to go without things, certainly not for any reason so trivial as war.

'What's all the mystery?' Susan asked pleasantly, sitting down and offering Norma a cigarette which Norma refused.

'No mystery, my dear, I've had a letter from Maurice.'

Susan flushed. 'He had no business to write to you.'

'That's what I thought, but he seems distressed at the idea of a divorce. *Did* you ask for one?'

'You seem to know all about it. Yes, I did.'

'Would you like to tell me about it, or shall I mind my own business?'

'I may as well tell you, then you'll know what it's all about. No doubt you'll be writing to Maurice anyway. However, this is in strict confidence.'

'I'm not sure I've any business accepting your confidences, Susan. I don't want to, but if I can help . . .'

'Perhaps you can,' Susan said. 'You might make that wretched husband of mine see reason.'

Norma wondered just which of them it was who was lacking in reason. She listened to Susan's brief account of what had happened at Christmas in Cirencester. She had met a man. His name was Harvey Orton and he was a neighbour of Lady Alys and her husband, Jasper Williams. He was a farmer and a fine horseman. They were in love and wished to marry. She had written to Maurice to ask for the evidence so she could divorce him, but she had not said there was another man. She saw no need. Maurice's behaviour was sufficient reason. She told the story with a quiet dignity but it seemed to Norma that there were a number of gaps in it.

'Haven't you seen Harvey Orton since last Christmas? That's almost a year,' she remarked.

'Of course I've seen him. I went to Warneford – that's his house – at Easter, and he came up during the summer.'

'Came up to Grunaglack? Was that wise?'

'Not to Grunaglack. He stayed in Fort William at a hotel. We met.'

'I see. How old is he?' Norma wondered why he had not been conscripted.

'He's twenty-seven. I know what you're thinking, but he's unfit for service.'

Norma frowned. She was thinking that Orton was four years younger than Susan whereas Lord Maurice was ten years older. Was that what lay behind this sudden infatuation for another man?

'He's not married, is he?'

'No, he lives alone at Warneford. He has no brothers or sisters, his father is dead and his mother remarried and went to Canada with her second husband.'

'You definitely want to marry him?'

'Yes I do. What did Maurice say to you in his letter?'

'Not a great deal. He simply said you'd written to say you wanted to divorce him and that he wouldn't hear of it. His exact words were, "Everything will look different after the war. For the boys' sakes I cannot countenance divorce." '

'The hypocrite. What about him and that promiscuous little secretary?'

Why was the secretary 'little', Norma wondered, apropos of nothing?

'Susan, what happened about Maurice and that secretary? You told me you were going to threaten to write to the Ambassador.'

'I told Maurice just what I thought of him. I also told him that if I heard any more gossip I'd complain direct to the Ambassador and that the scandal had reached England. I must say it worked,' she added with smug satisfaction.

'Worked in what way?' Norma enquired.

'Linda Bateman told me that all the gossip stopped quite suddenly. It seems Maurice took the hint.'

Or else became twice as careful as before, Norma mused. It surprised her that anyone could be as stupid as Susan, who calmly expected Maurice to allow her to divorce him when she herself was playing a most dangerous game.

'Why did Maurice write to you?' Susan demanded abruptly.

'Well may you ask,' Norma smiled wryly. 'He said I'm the matriarch of the family, as though that meant anything. Anyway he did write and he said that I was to impress on you that divorce is out of the question. I think he expects me to try to talk you round.'

'Mph,' Susan snorted.

'Quite so,' Norma agreed placidly. 'I have no intention of trying to influence anyone.'

'A divorce is the best thing for the boys' sake. If I go on seeing Harvey, as I have been doing, someone is bound to talk eventually – and you know how unpleasant that can be.'

Norma thought of the two Blood boys, Vernon aged ten and Philip aged eight. They were completely under their mother's influence. It would be interesting to know just what Susan said to them in private about their father. Norma, who liked children as a general rule, found it hard to get to know the two Blood boys. They were a little too perfect, too unreal to be natural. Like everything else in Susan's life, they were for show.

'What are you going to do?' Susan asked.

'I suppose I shall have to acknowledge Maurice's letter. I think I shall say I have spoken to you and that I propose to let you answer him yourself on the subject of divorce since I can't influence you.'

'That's right.' Susan looked satisfied and gave a triumphant little smile.

'You know,' Norma went on, 'it seems to me that you hardly know this Harvey Orton. The war appears to affect everyone, to make us rush into things in a way we wouldn't do ordinarily. Why don't you take your time over this, Susan?'

'I shall have to, shan't I?'

'I hope you know what you're doing,' Norma said.

'I love Harvey,' Susan said complacently.

'What does he do? Farm, did you say?'

'Yes, he has a farm. Not a very big one, but it's nice, and there's a lovely old house built of Cotswold stone.'

'It sounds attractive.'

'It is.'

'What would happen to the children if you were to divorce Maurice?' Norma asked.

'They'll be going to Eton in a year or two. They'd be able to see Maurice from time to time.'

'You'd expect them to make Mr Orton's farm their home, would you?'

'Of course. Maurice can't bring up children when he's overseas, can he? Besides, there's the matter of his morals.'

Norma wondered if the day would ever come when Susan would be unable to surprise her.

'Suppose Maurice means what he says, and you can't get a divorce?'

'He can't be so cruel. I'll have to think about that, but I'm not giving up Harvey and I don't see why I should give Maurice grounds against me, not after his behaviour. I'd write to the Foreign Secretary, and this time I mean it.'

'Things aren't quite the same now, are they?' Norma suggested.

'Why not?' Susan demanded, her mind busy with all the possibilities.

'Last time you threatened Maurice, you were the poor little wronged wife, living in the remote Highlands, bringing up your two innocent children. According to you Maurice was playing fast and loose while he was separated from you. Now you yourself say there is no scandal about him . . .'

'It doesn't alter the fact that there was scandal,' Susan interrupted tartly.

'. . . and now you're the one playing fast and loose.' She saw the change of expression on Susan's face. 'I'm sorry, but I must ask you to consider whether it is wise to wreck a marriage which is twelve years old on account of a man you hardly know.'

'You don't know Harvey.'

I'd like to, Norma thought grimly. There was something about the affair which sounded a jarring note. She did not like the sound of Harvey Orton at all – which was really very unfair as she knew nothing of him at first hand.

'Harvey is a friend of Maurice's sister.'

'Oh yes, so he is. Does Lady Alys know about you both?'

'I doubt it. I haven't discussed it. Until today I thought it was my own business.'

'If that refers to me, please believe me when I say I don't wish to interfere. I feel quite awkward.'

'I'm sorry,' Susan had the grace to apologize. 'I'm very upset.'

'Susan, there's just one thing. I know you have hardly any money of your own, so Harvey Orton can support you, can he? It isn't cheap to send two boys to Eton.'

'Harvey wouldn't pay for that. That's Maurice's business.'

'Yes, but you don't live very modestly, do you? You like to maintain a certain style.'

'We could manage.'

There was something defiant in her tone and Norma knew then that Harvey Orton was probably as hard up as Susan. She knew the type almost at once – he would have his hunters, his car, his country house, probably a butler before the war, and he'd have unpaid bills at the best tailoring establishment in London and at the local grocer's, and he'd dread letters from his bank manager. She sighed.

'Do think about it carefully before you commit yourself,' she urged.

'Yes, you've given me your good advice,' Susan snapped.

'So I have. Let's drop the subject,' Norma answered equally sharply.

'I must go. I have things to do. How is Alasdair?'

'Not much better.'

'I was sorry to hear how badly hurt he was.'

'We all are. Thank you for coming, Susan. I shan't interfere, you know.'

'It wouldn't do much good if you did. Give my love to Alasdair, won't you?'

She left and Norma went back into the drawing room to sit down at her desk and write a brief note to Maurice in Washington. She offered neither opinion nor advice but confined herself to fact, saying that Susan seemed determined and that she herself could do nothing. Lord Maurice would have to find some way of persuading Susan to wait till they could meet and discuss it properly, if indeed that was what he wanted.

It was not a very good letter, Norma thought as she put it out for posting on the tray in the hall, but it was the best she could do. Maurice would have to fight this battle himself. What he would say or do if he discovered Susan was having an affair of her own, heaven only knew.

One evening towards the end of January, 1944, Ipla answered the telephone and told Fiona it was a call for her. Fiona guessed it might be Norman and wondered why he was phoning.

'I called to say goodbye,' he told her abruptly.

'Goodbye?' She felt a sudden fear clutch her heart.

'Yes, I'm off to the south of England. I've got my posting.'

'When?' she asked fearfully.

'I leave in the morning. I thought I'd let you know. I wasn't going to and then I thought it would be churlish to sneak away without a word. You don't mind do you?'

'No.' There was a catch in her voice. 'Thank you for calling.'

'How's . . . your husband?'

'Just the same. He doesn't get any better. It's going to be a long business. He sees the doctor once a week.'

'I'm sorry, Fiona.'

'Will you be going overseas?'

'I don't know. Not right away, I shouldn't think.'

'If you go, will you tell me?'

'Yes, if that's what you want.'

'It's what I want.' She sighed. 'Oh, Norman.'

'I know.' His voice was flat, emotionless. 'Goodbye, Fiona.'

He hung up before she could speak. She put down the phone slowly and felt tears pricking at her eyelids. It was so unfair, she thought. She went back into the sitting room where Alasdair sat by the fire, a book open but ignored on his knee. Norma was upstairs in her room and the children were in the library where they were ostensibly doing some homework.

'Who was it?' Alasdair asked as Fiona came back into the room.

'One of the officers from Lochailort. I've known him for quite a long time. He's been posted.'

'Do I know him?'

'You met him. A Captain Windsor.'

'I don't remember him properly. Has he been up here long?'

'Since some time in 1941.'

'Lucky fellow, spending his war here.'

'Not any more.'

'No, of course not. Those commandos are quite a tough lot. If I hadn't been with the regiment, I'd have liked to be a commando myself.'

'Didn't you do enough?' she asked sharply.

'What's enough? Your friend Windsor became a commando and he's spent years up here enjoying himself. Somebody else becomes a cook and a shell lands on the cookhouse and he's killed or maimed. You take your chance.'

'If men stayed at home and women ran industry and Government, there'd be no wars,' she said heatedly.

'I don't blame you for being angry with us.'

'I wonder if any of you have any idea of the suffering and misery caused by war? I don't just mean the killed and the wounded, but the people who knew them. Everyone is touched by it.'

'I know it must be hard for you,' he sighed. 'You haven't had much fun since we married, have you? First there was all that separation while I was in India and you had to come home because of your health, and then came this war. It's turned out badly. I don't blame you if you're bitter.'

'Seeing you makes me bitter.'

'It shouldn't,' he answered gently. 'I wouldn't mind too much if I didn't feel so ill and have these funny spells. They're terrible while they last, then they go away suddenly and I feel normal again. Losing an arm isn't too awful and perhaps I'll get something done about my face when I feel better. I can even stand the loss of my career – I never had to live on my Army pay anyway, and there's always Al to make up for it – but what I can't stomach is feeling wretchedly ill four or five or six times a day.'

He'd never been ill in his life and she could see that he was as frustrated as she was, if for a different reason. Why couldn't the doctors do anything to help? He'd had to put off his visit to London to receive his Victoria Cross from the King because he wasn't fit to travel so far.

'I don't know what I'd do without you,' he said unexpectedly.

'Why? I don't do anything,' she countered, feeling guilty.

'You're here, and that's what matters. I'm very selfish, Fiona. I think only of myself. You're too young to be tied to a cripple. If you wanted to go away . . . I'd understand.'

Oh don't, she cried silently. *Don't make it worse than it it is already.*

'Did you hear me?' he asked after a few moments.

'Yes. Don't be silly, darling. Of course I shan't go away.'

'You won't be thirty till August. You're too young for this sort of thing. A holiday is what you need.'

'A holiday from what? I don't work except to help Norma in the house and the grounds.'

'A holiday from that then.'

'Stop being so miserable,' she told him, mustering a smile. 'You'll get over these spells of feeling ill, and then we'll both go away for a holiday. I don't mind your face very much, darling, but for your own sake you should have something done. It will only make you morbid if you leave it as it is.'

'All right. Later. Perhaps this summer, or next. There's no hurry. It will mean going away for several weeks.'

'I know. Dr Macpherson in Inverness told me all about it.'

He changed the subject. 'It's funny young Al has become so bitter about the Army, as though it were the regiment which wounded me, not the Germans. I hope he'll get over it. I thought he'd be pleased about the V.C.'

'He's like all children. He thought war was a game till he saw what it did to you.'

'I'm alive aren't I? I had a good war, really.'

A good war she thought, staring at the fire. Probably he meant it. Promotion and medals made it a good war. Norma had been right when she had said once that Alasdair and his father were like children who never grew up. Their dream was of military glory, their God a Highland regiment. 'Peter Pan in a kilt,' was how Norma had described her husband. It was so apt. A good war! Really . . . it was enough to make one cry.

'Thank God for Al,' he said suddenly after several minutes' silence in which his thoughts had ranged far and wide.

'Why do you say that, dear?' she asked.

'I was thinking of the family. There's no one at Ardclune except women, and the two boys at Grunaglack aren't MacInneses at all, they're Bloods. My grandfather would be shocked if he knew. Even here there's only myself and the boy, but it's better than nothing.'

'Alasdair, I hope you aren't counting on Pal Al going to Sandhurst,' she said.

'Why not? You mean because of his attitude to my wounds? That will change. He's only a child.'

'He's a very impressionable child and he may not change at all. Sometimes childhood prejudices last for ever. They aren't easy to eradicate and he's been deeply shocked.'

'He's been talking to you?'

'Yes. I told him he was too young to worry about what he'd do when he grows up.'

'I always knew what I'd do. Always.'

'You're a very uncomplicated person, darling. Pal Al isn't. He asks a lot of questions about life.'

'What do you mean? What sort of questions?'

'Why some people are rich and some are poor, why we

send criminals to prison – he seems to think it's rather a silly thing to do. For a nine-year-old he's very complicated. He'll surprise us all, I'm sure. That's why I don't want *you* to find consolation for your own disappointment in dreams of Al becoming a General. He's just as likely to become a politician.'

He reacted as she thought he would. 'Not that, anything but that. I can't stand politicians.'

She smiled. As she had said, he was uncomplicated.

'Then be prepared for anything, darling.'

'A fine cheerful sort of person you are,' he grumbled, but he was smiling. 'I'll say it again, what would I do without you? I wish I could tell you what a difference it has made being married to you. I don't think you know.'

She didn't and she realized it. Sometimes she wondered why he had bothered marrying at all, yet she believed him. In his own way he obviously adored her. She thought of Norman, and bit her lip. It would have been far better if she'd never met Norman Windsor. It was something else to blame on the war, the interminable war. When would it all end? And how?

May came home to Castlemore for a visit during April. She had changed a lot and looked older than her age, yet she was full of a quiet courage of her own.

'Are you on holiday?' Norma asked her.

'No, the doctor suggested sick leave. As a matter of fact I feel rather low at the moment. Teddy has gone to India.'

'Teddy? Edward Gentle?'

'Yes of course.' May laughed. 'Did you think I collected men like antiques? He's getting a divorce. We gave his wife evidence and she's petitioned. It's just our damned bad luck his being sent off like this. It means we'll have to wait years till he comes home before we can marry.'

'Poor May. I'm sorry. Whereabout is he?'

'He's at Air Headquarters in New Delhi. I had a letter and he seems well and happy enough. It's a staff job. At least he's safe.'

'Then you're lucky,' Norma pointed out.

'Yes I know. I was very lucky to meet Teddy in the first place, after Boy's death. I thought I'd never get over that. I'm a fool really, becoming miserable like this, but sometimes I'm quite sorry for myself. I hate waiting.'

'We all do. What are your plans now?'

'I don't know. I'll go back to Weobley anyway. I'd rather like to work in a factory.'

'A factory!' Norma blinked in surprise.

'Yes. I feel such a fraud doing nothing to help the war along. Other women have to work on farms or in factories, why shouldn't I?'

'If they want you they'll call you up. Anyway, wouldn't a farm be better?'

'Much better.'

'I don't understand.'

'Don't you think some of the men in Burma or North Africa or Italy wouldn't rather have a nice time down on the farm? Somebody has to work in factories. It might do me good. I've been spoiled all my life.'

'What a strange person you are. I used to worry about you, but I have a feeling that you don't need anyone to worry.'

'I hope not. How is everything here?'

Norma gave her all the family news. Alasdair had been worse than usual and he was going to Inverness in a few days' time to see a specialist and to have a series of tests carried out. Dr Macpherson was worried about him. If it had been strain which had been causing the dizzy spells and the bouts of illness, there ought to have been an improvement by now. He wasn't satisfied with the tests which had been carried out earlier when Alasdair came home from the Desert. There was an excellent man at Raigmore in Inverness.

'Poor Alasdair. He must be miserable at being out of the war.'

'He is. It's a strain on Fiona too.'

'I suppose so.' May didn't sound very sincere. She still remembered how Fiona had spoken to Boy Loring, and she had never quite forgiven her for it.

'It is, May,' Norma said quietly. 'I don't think she even loves him.'

'What?' May leaned forwards. 'What do you mean, Mama?'

'It's just an impression I have. She loved him all right when they were married in 1934, but that's a long time ago and there's been a lot of separation. I think the first flush of romance has worn away and left nothing underneath. Don't please say anything, but sometimes I believe Fiona is living in a sort of private hell. Perhaps it's just my imagination.'

'No,' May said, shaking her head. 'Perhaps not. Come to think of it, Alasdair would be a very unsatisfactory husband.'

'Like his father,' Norma smiled. 'Not many women would have put up with Dair as cheerfully as I did. It isn't much fun playing second fiddle to a lot of soldiers. Hairy fairies, Charles used to call them,' she added with a laugh.

'This is heresy coming from you,' May told her.

'Do you think I have no feeling, no personality of my own?' Norma laughed quietly. 'I'm a very happy person, but I'm not stupid. Sometimes I ask myself if I haven't sacrificed a husband and a son for nothing. I don't mean that I have any regrets or that I am not tremendously proud of them both, merely that I find myself questioning my values now. It's a very uncomfortable process.'

'Good lord, what brought about this change?'

'Alasdair, of course. When he came home so badly hurt I began to think again about everything in life. What got me on to this theme? It's having you to talk to, that's what it is. You were never one to tolerate sacred cows.'

'I must have been a sore trial to you,' Mary laughed.

'No, you weren't. Oh yes, about Fiona – be nice to her, please May. Something is upsetting her. Life isn't easy.'

'I suppose not. Thanks for warning me. I'd never have thought about it otherwise.'

'You should go and visit Leona. She's lonely and Finvola isn't much company for her.'

'I don't mind Leona but I'm not keen to meet Finvola,' May laughed. 'Anyway I'll go. How is Susan?'

'In England, visiting friends.'

'She gets around, doesn't she, war or no war?'

Norma nodded. Susan was staying with Harvey Orton, but no one in the family knew anything about it. The secret was well kept.

May got up and sat on the arm of her mother's chair. She put an arm round the older woman's shoulder and kissed her forehead.

'What's that for?' Norma asked, pleased.

'What do you think? Why do you imagine I put up with the horrible journey here by train? Too see you, of course. There's a phrase Boy used to use quite a lot when we were first married. It fits perfectly.'

'What's that?'

'I came to see you to charge my batteries. Somehow or other when things aren't too good, we can all draw strength from you. I wonder where you draw it from?'

'From all of you, of course,' Norma answered, her heart swelling with happiness.

9

Captain Norman Windsor shifted in his seat and ruffled the pages of the letter he had just read. It was a very sad letter and he re-read it carefully before putting it back in its envelope.

'Darling,

'You probably wonder why I am writing so soon after you have left us here, but there is news of my husband. Our family doctor was not at all pleased with his progress, or to be more exact his lack of it, so he sent him to Raigmore Hospital in Inverness where they carried out a number of tests. We have now heard what is wrong with Alasdair, and it is nothing to do with the war or his wounds at all. It is something that would have happened even if he had remained safely at home. Norman, he has leukaemia and he is going to die, quite soon I think. Nothing can save him. At the moment he is at home but eventually, in a month, perhaps two months, he will have to go into hospital, and he will never come out.

'It is such a cruel fate, and there is nothing anyone can do to help. He knows. He insisted on knowing and whatever else one can say about Alasdair, one has to admit his courage, moral as well as physical. You can imagine what life here is like. The children don't know, and won't until the last moment.

'Why is it that having suffered so much in battle, and survived despite the odds against survival, he should come home to die like this? Are you religious? I'm not. I find it impossible to believe in a God who is supposed to love me personally. The old Norse Gods are much easier to understand.

'How fortunate it is that we decided to wait and not face Alasdair with the truth about ourselves. Can you imagine him having to bear that burden as well? I am still stunned by the news – I have been going round in a daze since I heard. I meant to write to you ten days ago, when I first heard, but I have kept postponing it. I simply didn't want to make the effort. I keep hoping I'll go to bed one night and wake up next morning back at home in Castle Fearn, young and unmarried, that all this is some sort of nasty dream and will go away. Of course it isn't. Thank God you're not a dream.

'Think of me sometimes, Norman, and when all this is over come back to see me if you still wish to and we can talk about the future where there *is* a future. I do hope you are well. I don't know where you are or what you're doing, but being a commando I have no doubt you are often in danger. I wish I could say or do something to help. All I can do is to say thank you. You gave me something I needed, when I needed it, and I shall never stop loving you whatever happens to us.'

He sat in a deep leather armchair in the ante-room of the long low wooden building which was their Officers' Mess. His handsome face was sombre and he ignored the whisky and soda at his elbow. He was in the very peak of physical condition, and he knew that some time soon the big show was going to start. The invasion of Europe was not far off. He knew that his commando would be in the thick of it and that casualties would be high. What an ironic business war was. What stupid pranks it played on people. When it was over, if he happened to survive, he knew what he was going to write about – he was going to write about the sort of men who caused wars, and he was going to do his damndest to make sure that there was never another war. That was his plain duty.

148

He glanced at the letter again. How she suffered, and how helpless he was to give her comfort or hope. He wondered how on earth he could reply to her letter. It would not be easy. If fact it would be far better if he could see her and talk to her instead of having to try to put it all down in writing.

'Snap out of it, chum. It can't be as bad as all that.'

He looked up and saw one of his friends, a young Major with the D.S.O.

'Come on, Norman. Bring your drink up to the bar. What's wrong? Has the popsie given you the old heave-ho?'

'No, not quite.' He managed to grin.

'A woman should be like a good drink, old boy. Tempting enough to make you want another.'

'You're a cynic,' Norman said, tucking the letter into the breast pocket of his battledress blouse and getting up from his chair.

'A thirsty one, and that's a frightful combination. It's your turn to pay, you know.'

Fiona, going through each day in a daze, wondered if she had done the right thing in writing to Norman. Was she being selfish, trying to have her cake and eat it too? Was she being disloyal to her dying husband? They were cruel questions to attempt to answer. She had no idea how long it would take for her letter to reach Norman, or for his reply to come to her – always assuming that he would reply. Perhaps he had found someone else by now, someone unmarried, someone more vivacious, not a miserable creature like herself.

Alasdair, strangely enough, was much more cheerful now that he knew he was dying. It was as though he was determined to make the utmost of every hour. It was only during his attacks that his unseen malady got the better of him. They went out in the car as often as they could, and he was taking an interest in the garden and suggested to Norma that they build a high-walled rose walk beside the fountain. They spent hours with catalogues planning the rose walk but the trouble was building the walls. At least it kept them amused, discussing it.

When at last Norman's letter reached her, it cheered Fiona up tremendously although it was very short.

'I simply don't know what to write so I shan't even try,' it said. 'God knows I wish I could comfort you. I love you Fiona and I always will. I shall come back to Castlemore as soon as ever I can. You know that, don't you, darling? It's going to be all right, really it is. This is short because I don't want to say the wrong thing. The right thing to say is "I love you." I do, you know. Keep writing when you can.'

The few lines meant the world to her. She felt she could play out her part with Alasdair. He would never know that in her heart she had betrayed him long ago while he was in North Africa. He would never guess.

At the end of June, Susan arrived unannounced one morning while Fiona and Alasdair were out. Norma received her coolly and they walked in the garden until tea was brought out to the summer house.

'I feel such a fool,' Susan blurted out when Norma had poured tea.

'Why is that, my dear?'

'Over that scoundrel, Harvey Orton, of course.'

Norma paused for a fraction of a second and then raised her cup and drank.

'What happened?' she asked.

'He's in debt up to his ears, of course. He tried to borrow five thousand pounds from me. After all I've done for him.'

'You have?'

'I didn't mean to say, but yes, I've given him five hundred pounds. I should have known. Alys and Jasper

Williams have been bitten too. They lent him five hundred as well.'

'What exactly has he done with all this money?'

'Gone to London. He's put the farm up for sale. Oh damn it.' She swore lustily.

'Tell me about it from the beginning,' Norma said.

It wasn't a complicated tale. Susan had gone down to Warneford to spend a week with him. Maurice was still being awkward over a divorce and they had been talking of living together as man and wife, unmarried. Susan had always assumed that he had plenty of money because of the way he spent, and when he had asked her to lend him five hundred pounds for something to do with the farm, because he was caught short of ready cash and didn't want to sell any of his share portfolio, she had given him the money gladly even though if left her bank balance very low. On this last visit he had begun by inviting her to take the plunge and become Mrs Orton in name if not in legal fact. She had even agreed, and then he had said casually that he'd need five thousand to settle his debts and set them up together. That was when he learned that her money all came from Maurice and that she had only a few thousand pounds of her own which she had no intention of touching. She learned also that he had been living on diminishing credit for years. It turned out that he had got through quite a modest fortune gambling most of his money away at horse racing. They had had a furious quarrel and she had wakened up next morning to find herself in sole occupancy of Warneford. He had left a note saying that he had gone to London and she could contact him at his club *if* she could help with money. If she could borrow five thousand from her husband he was sure they'd be all right because he was on to some sure-fire money-making scheme.

She had gone to Jasper Williams at once to find out what he knew about Harvey Orton, and Williams told her that he had lent Orton five hundred pounds. In the end she had returned, defeated, to Grunaglack. If she was richer in experience she was considerably lighter in the pocket.

'What's your problem?' Norma asked impatiently. She had far more serious things to worry about than Susan's wild extravagances and their consequences. 'You seem to me to be very lucky. Just think if you'd gone off with him *before* you found out all this.'

'What am I to tell Maurice?' Susan wailed.

'I should tell him you're sorry,' Norma replied promptly. 'You'd better make it up with him.'

'He'll be furious.'

'I hardly think so. Just say you've changed your mind and that you don't want a divorce. That's all. Don't do anything stupid like saying you loved him all the time. He won't believe you. You've got a nice home, a titled husband, a certain amount of money, two healthy sons – try counting your blessings for a change, Susan, instead of always thinking how somebody else is so much better off than you are.'

'Alys and her husband should have warned me.'

'It sounds as though they got caught too, so how could they warn you? Anyway they didn't ask you to become infatuated with Orton, did they?'

'It's all very well for you to sound smug. I feel a fool.'

'Susan dear, you *are* a fool. The day you realize that, there is hope for you.'

'Well, *really*!'

'What did you expect – that I'd hold your hand? Don't be ridiculous. You're a grown woman who's behaved like a schoolgirl. You're well out of it.'

'Who are you to talk?' Susan asked unexpectedly. 'You were engaged to your husband's brother and nearly had an illegitimate baby.'

Norma looked at her steadily. 'There was never any question of having an illegitimate baby,' she replied coolly, 'but I take your point. If you feel like that, what

152

are you doing here, Susan? I didn't invite you. I've never pried into your affairs. You and Maurice both came to me.'

'I'm sorry.' Susan coloured. 'I didn't mean what I said. I'm upset.'

'But I meant what I said, Susan. It's time you realized that you are a fool. For years you've given yourself airs and graces until you were no longer content with your husband – you wanted a younger one, a newer model. Now an unscrupulous man has taken advantage of you. If you'd concentrated on being a good wife and a good mother none of this would have happened. I'm sorry if you think I've no right to preach, but I'm older than you are, and I'm giving you the benefit of my experience. I don't feel superior to anyone, believe me.'

'It's going to be difficult writing to Maurice,' Susan muttered, deciding to abandon the topic of her own folly.

'I've given you my advice. Just say you've changed your mind about divorce. When is he coming home, anyway?'

'I don't know. With this war nobody knows anything any more. I suppose they'll keep him there for the duration.'

She left shortly afterwards without having mentioned Alasdair's name. It was a typical oversight, Norma thought. Susan would never really change her spots but at least she might make the effort and try to behave less selfishly.

The same day brought a visit from Leona who had had to go to Fort William and decided to come on to Castlemore. Her news was that Rajah Sahib was coming home for a month's holiday soon. Norma had always liked Leona, not least because she was so plainly in love with her tall, dark husband. There was something refreshingly pleasant about the way Leona talked about him, not fulsomely, but quite simply as though he were the centre of the universe.

'How are you coping with Finvola?' Norma asked her.

'Not badly now.' Leona laughed. 'She's really very kind when you get to know her. I've discovered what her trouble is.'

'What?'

'She hates men. Quite literally. She has a thing about them. Talk about one of nature's spinsters!' Leona chuckled delightedly. 'I'm sure she'll be absolutely disgusted when Rajah comes home and we share the same bedroom. She'd much prefer him to sleep on the top floor in an attic, and not be seen at all.'

'But I thought she rescued drunken sailors in London or something.'

'She did, and that's the point. She loved it because it confirmed her view that all men are unspeakable beasts, not really human beings at all. I'm so glad I've got two daughters. She fusses over Eve and Mary, but if they'd been boys she'd probably make them sleep outside in dog kennels. It's very simple really.'

'I wonder what made her like that,' Norma said.

'Goodness knows. Not my mother and father, I'm certain. Did you ever meet a nicer man than my father?'

'No.' Norma remembered Wee Ken, gentle, humorous, the soul of kindness.

'Anyway I get along very well with Finvola, now that I've got her measure, which makes a pleasant change. Incidentally, between ourselves, she has no time for Susan at all.'

'Oh dear, poor Susan. What's she done?'

'I don't know. Something she said, I think. Anyway Finvola sniffs mightily every time Susan's name comes up, which isn't often. We're quite a mad family, really.'

'We are a family, and that's what counts.'

'You always say the right thing, don't you?' Leona said with admiration.

'My dear, how I wish that were true.'

These little encounters with the rest of the clan provided momentary diversions for Norma, but nothing could dispell the chill hand that lay over Castlemore. There was a special problem, for when Alasdair had to go into hospital they would take him to Inverness, on the other side of the county. Travel would be awkward enough to be impossible. If they were going to be with him they would have to stay in a hotel there, and this raised all sorts of questions about the children. Deirdre had offered to look after them until she had to go back to university, but although Alasdair could not live for long, the disease was unpredictable. It could be four weeks or four months. His time in hospital could be a few days or several weeks.

Meantime Alasdair actually seemed to be better, part of the time. They did not know of the awful pain that seemed to cut him in two from time to time, this thing that turned his life into a torment for brief periods. All they knew was that he appeared more gay, more sprightly. His courage shamed them. He never referred to his illness, never made it an excuse. When he had one of his turns he managed to get up to his room and sweat it out in silence. Only occasionally did it catch him on the hop and when it did he would crouch in a chair, lips tightly sealed, waiting for it to pass.

In the end he did not go to hospital at all. He defied death until the last moment. On the morning of the 14th of August, which was Fiona's thirtieth birthday, he went to the bathroom first thing in the morning to wash and shave. It was only when he had been gone for twenty minutes that Fiona became suspicious and went to look for him. He was lying dead on the floor.

Although nobody ever admitted it aloud, and none of them even liked to admit it to themselves silently, Alasdair's death was a release for them all. Nothing had been right since he had come home from North Africa.

He was buried in the churchyard at Fort William where other members of the family lay. Almost at once the question arose of his Victoria Cross, which still had to be presented. Norma wrote to the Colonel of the regiment, General Sir Donald MacDonald, and asked if it could be presented privately as they did not want to attend an ordinary investiture. His widow and son, she explained, were prostrated by their grief at Alasdair's untimely death.

It was quickly arranged and Fiona, Pal Al and Frances Mary travelled to London together where the King received them privately in Buckingham Palace and handed over the supreme award for gallantry in the face of the enemy to Pal Al, who wore his best kilt for the occasion. No journalists knew what was going on and they were able to leave as privately as they had come, and to return directly to Castlemore. Pal Al had handed the velvet-lined case to his mother once they were out in the Palace courtyard.

'You have it,' he said, quite composed. 'I don't want it.' He sounded older than his nine years.

'Don't you, darling? He was your father.'

'That's not my father in that box,' he flashed back quickly. 'That's just a stupid medal.'

Silently Fiona tucked the box into her handbag, and when she got home she gave it to Norma.

'You've got all your husband's things, so you might as well have Alasdair's. At the moment Pal Al isn't interested in them.'

Norma nodded. There was an attic where she kept all sorts of mementoes of the family. Now she added her son's medals, and the sword which somehow had become a symbol to her. It occurred to her that if Pal Al maintained his attitude she could hand everything over to the Military Museum in Edinburgh one day. There was no hurry. They already had some of Dair's things, and the regiment had a few others.

When they looked into Alasdair's affairs they found out that, as Kenneth had once privately feared, he had *all* his money in Ranitser. And the shares were well down, even with the war boosting similar shares. His estate was a mere £20,000 and went to Fiona. Fiona was well content, but Norma was astonished when she discovered that their son had broken the family tradition of sound investment and put all his money into anything as speculative as Ranitser.

Fiona wrote to Norman Windsor who had been in Europe ever since the D-Day landings early in June. He had won an M.C. at Caen on the 9th of June and was now a Major, a promotion which he regarded as hilariously funny considering he was a journalist and a most reluctant soldier. They wrote regularly now and Alasdair was not mentioned in their letters. That was a closed chapter in her life. They had the future to consider.

Deirdre spent quite a lot of time at Ardclune that summer. Eve was getting ready to enter Miss Weir's in Perth as a boarder and was as excited as only a nine-year-old can be. The prospect of going to boarding school did not daunt her at all. Going to Miss Weir's was part of the process of growing up in the family, and it would put her streets ahead of her younger sister Mary, who would have to wait a whole year to follow her to Perth. Deirdre had promised to take Eve to Perth, much to Leona's delight. Eve had started to hero-worship her cousin, which was no bad thing. Even Finvola liked Deirdre, rather to Norma's surprise. Leona had explained it privately to Norma by saying that Deirdre's illegitimacy was the living proof that all men were beasts. This kept Norma amused for some time when Leona passed it on. Finvola had become the 'character' of the family, the eccentric without which no family seemed to be complete.

One morning when Norma was down first she collected

the mail from the hall and took Fiona's up to her room.

'Another Forces letter,' she remarked, handing it over. 'Is it that young Lieutenant Windsor?'

'He's a Major now. How did you guess?'

'I knew there was something between the two of you. One night when I couldn't sleep I saw you going to the summer house, and he followed. I wasn't snooping, I happened to be sitting at my window, that's all.' She did not add that the summer house had special memories for her.

'I see.'

'I was afraid you'd leave Alasdair. You love Major Windsor, don't you?'

'Yes. You're very perceptive. I'd hoped I had managed to conceal it.'

'You did, I'm certain of it. I stumbled on your secret by accident.'

'You aren't angry?' Fiona asked.

'Why should I be, my dear? You're human. It was no fun for you being married to my son. I'm very grateful that you kept your secret from him. It might have broken his heart.'

'I know. Norman has been very patient.'

'Do you plan to marry him now?'

'I don't know. Honestly we haven't discussed the future. The war, you know.'

'Yes, I do know. Fiona, can I say something?'

'You know you can.'

'I want you to be happy – you must believe that – but there's Pal Al.'

'What of him?'

'I don't think he'll ever join the Army. I have a feeling about it, one which you share I know. Perhaps it is as well his father didn't live to see it come to pass. However he is a MacInnes, and Castlemore will be his. I wouldn't want him to be taken away from here if it could be avoided.'

'I hadn't thought of that.'

'I only had one son, and you've only got one son. It would be a tragedy if Castlemore passed out of the family. This is Pal Al's heritage.'

'I understand. I'll write to Norman about it. We will arrange something.'

'You don't think I'm interfering?'

'No.' Fiona put her arms round Norma. 'How could I think that? You're very kind to me, very understanding.'

'I try to understand,' Norma agreed. 'It doesn't always work. I'll never understand Susan fully if I live to be a hundred.'

'I hope you will live to be a hundred. I don't know what Norman's plans are for after the war, but Al will go to Lamond's in Pitlochry and spend his holidays here. I can promise that much. I'll try to make him understand about Castlemore.'

'Thank you my dear.'

In September a heartbroken letter arrived from May in Weobley. In it she told her mother that Wing Commander Gentle had died on the 3rd of the month in a military hospital in New Delhi. He had been struck down quite suddenly by meningitis. He had named her as his next of kin, although his divorce had not been finalized, so his personal effects were being sent to her. Luckily he had made a will leaving all his money to his wife, and this had not been changed, so one source of possible unpleasantness had been avoided. May was selling her cottage in Weobley because it had too many unpleasant memories. She would like to come home to Castlemore. Was it all right?

Norma replied at once saying that there was plenty of room for her. When was she coming? The answer was that she was coming at once. She arrived early in October. The cottage was unsold, and she had simply left it in the hands of a Hereford agent. There were enormous dark rings under her eyes, and at first she seemed to have shrunk. She was quiet and unsmiling.

Castlemore was still a home from home for the officers at Lochailort, and there was now a standing invitation for six of them to come to lunch every Sunday. Somehow they managed to provide a passable buffet lunch, and even occasionally a more formal meal, and there was a very special relationship between the house and the commando school. People in England, the United States, Australia, Canada and New Zealand, some of whom had never visited Scotland, heard in letters about Castlemore and the woman who presided over the family there. Above the big stone fireplace in the hall of Castlemore there was a polished oak shield and on it a black triangle with a red dagger, which was now the commando badge. It had been made by some of the men at Lochailort, and Norma was enormously proud of it.

One of their most frequent visitors and best friends was a stocky little American who had been a film stunt man before the war. He had succeeded in coming over and joining the commandos before the United States entered the war, and thereafter had refused to be transferred back to the U.S. Army, saying that he was a goddamned commando and intended to stay one. He had been on early raids in Norway, and he had been at Dieppe, and survived them. The rest of the time he had been at Lochailort. He was much decorated and had a tremendous sense of humour. He was one of the few people who knew about Fiona and Norman Windsor, and he was a special friend of Fiona's. His name was Alan Edgerton and he had known many famous Hollywood film stars.

He was just the person to cheer up May, so Fiona told him all about May and Wing Commander Gentle.

'Leave it to me, Fiona,' Alan assured her confidently. 'I'll cheer up the poor kid. That's a terrible thing. Two husbands in one war.'

'She wasn't actually married to Edward Gentle,' Fiona reminded him.

'Same thing, same thing.'

He was about May's age and was as good as his word. Week-end after week-end he monopolized her and soon he had her smiling again. Fiona and Norma breathed a sigh of relief, until suddenly it dawned on them that the plan had worked more thoroughly than Fiona had bargained for. May had fallen in love with Alan Edgerton.

'How could she?' Norma asked Fiona when they were alone. 'She's had Boy and Edward Gentle. How can she go on falling in love like this?'

'She's on the rebound. Don't worry about it. Alan will handle her.'

'He's not married. Suppose he feels the same way about her?'

'Alan has too much sense,' Fiona assured her, but she wondered. Alan seemed to enjoy his task of cheering up May. Was he enjoying it more than he should? There was nothing any of them could do about it.

At Christmas they had a party at Castlemore. It was held on Boxing Day, which was a Tuesday, and about fifteen or sixteen officers from Lochailort rolled up at various times. Leona had come over, leaving the children for a few hours with Finvola, and even Susan put in an appearance. Everyone was very gay, for it really did seem now that the end of the war was in sight and that it might all be over within a year.

Deirdre, on holiday from Aberdeen, was especially pretty that day, and held a private court of her own with the younger officers. Norma marvelled at how easily she handled them, and at her self-confidence. She was twenty now, and not even the war and its restrictions could dull her infinite zest for life. Just before teatime she went into the passage behind the hall where there was a downstairs cloakroom. She was followed by rather a callow young officer with more muscle than brain, who had been drinking fairly freely and who considered correctly that Deirdre MacInnes was a gorgeous creature. As he put down his drink and followed her, he was noticed by Alan Edgerton, standing talking to May. Alan frowned. He knew the young man in question and was not much impressed at the best of times. He had no business going into that passage.

'Excuse me, Mary,' he said, putting down his own drink. 'I'll be back in a minute.'

She smiled at him and then as she saw where he was going, she frowned. She followed too. As she stepped through the doorway Alan grabbed her and pulled her to him, putting his finger to his lips. Further along the passage the tall young man, hands in pockets, waited impatiently for Deirdre. He did not have long to wait. She came out of the cloakroom and he stepped towards her.

'Hullo,' he greeted her.

'What are you doing here, Tom?' she asked.

'Waiting for you. There's too much company next door.'

He took her arm as he spoke and she pulled free. He scowled and grabbed at her.

'Come on, Deirdre, don't be stuffy. It's a party.'

Deirdre's response was automatic. As he put his hands where they had no business to be, she slapped him hard. That should have been the end of the matter. It was the sort of incident which was commonplace. The young officer was too full of his own importance and Norma's whisky, and also he considered himself an excellent answer to any maiden's prayer.

'Don't do that,' he snarled and pulled her towards him, his hands gripping her hard. 'Don't be such a prude. Let's have fun.'

Alan was already moving away from May. He was an expert in unarmed combat and his hands and his right knee did their business beautifully and swiftly. One young commando crumpled to the ground unconscious.

'Are you all right Deirdre?' Alan asked.

'Yes thanks. You arrived just in time.'

'I saw him following you so I tagged along. I had a hunch he wasn't invited.'

'Certainly not, the dirty-minded brute. Thanks for taking care of him.'

'My pleasure. Mary's over there. You two girls go back to the party and I'll remove this jerk the back way and dump him in one of the jeeps. Okay?'

He winked and took the unconscious officer outside where, in his own words to May later, he 'damaged him slightly in transit' before dumping him in the back of a vehicle. Deirdre's fun was not over, for within a quarter of an hour another commando, the son of a very wealthy industrialist and eminently eligible from the female point of view, proposed to her.

'But I've only met you today,' Deirdre answered, amazed.

'It doesn't matter,' he said seriously. 'I love you. We could get married by special licence.'

'I don't want to get married.'

'You don't? I'm serious you know. I can afford it, if that's what's worrying you.'

'Nothing is worrying me, believe me. Nothing at all.'

'You won't marry me?' he asked, as if not quite believing her.

'Definitely not. Thanks very much for asking.'

'I'm damned. You're the first girl I've ever asked.'

'You're almost the first man I've ever refused,' Deirdre replied with a laugh. 'We're both gaining experience.'

'It's a shame,' he said sadly. 'I shall become a Trappist monk after the war.'

When they had all gone back to Lochailort, apart from Alan Edgerton whom May had invited to stay on to dinner, Norma asked Deirdre if she had enjoyed herself.

'Yes, enormously. Someone wanted to rape me, someone else wanted to marry me.'

163

Norma looked at her uncertainly, but Deirdre's blue eyes were merry.

'Honestly. Alan dealt with the first and I dealt with the second.'

'Do you mean you were attacked? I won't have them back if they can't behave.'

'No, it's not as bad as that. He had too much to drink and became rather amorous. Luckily Alan was there and took care of him before there was any trouble. He won't do it again, believe me.'

'Perhaps it was a mistake having so many here. Usually I only invite a few but I thought we might have open house today.'

'It wasn't a mistake,' Deirdre said. 'Honestly. I had a lot of fun, and no harm was done. Just think, I've had my first real proposal.'

'What did you say?' Norma asked, her curiosity getting the better of her.

'I said I didn't want to get married. Do you know, I honestly think he expected me to accept him.'

'I'm glad you've got more sense.'

Deirdre kissed her.

'I shan't marry anyone unless you give me permission,' she said lightly. 'I wouldn't want a husband if you didn't approve of him.'

'When you find your happiness, take it with both hands and don't worry about other people. That's what I did,' Norma said gently.

'I'll remember, but I'm in no hurry to leave Castlemore,' Deirdre assured her.

IO

In January of 1945 May became officially engaged to Alan Edgerton, and even though they both said they would wait till the war was over before marrying, Norma was filled with foreboding. She confided in Fiona.

'If anything goes wrong this time, think of the effect on May. Oh Fiona, a commando of all people. He's so liable to get killed.'

'Yes,' Fiona agreed, thinking of Norman. She was worried about him constantly.

'It's the worst possible thing that could have happened.'

'Look on the bright side,' Fiona urged. 'The war might end quite soon now, and then everything will be all right. Don't you think May deserves her happiness?'

'I do, but I don't believe she can really have fallen in love with three different men so quickly – Boy, Edward Gentle and now Alan Edgerton. It doesn't make sense.'

'Not to you. You're a one-man woman. Others are different. I was in love with Alasdair when I married him and now I'm in love with Norman.'

'That's different too. You're a lot older now and it was a long time ago that you married Alasdair.'

'Owch,' Fiona said, smiling, and Norma apologized. 'I didn't mean it like that, but you haven't rushed from man to man as May's doing.'

'Don't worry. It will be all right and Alan's the nicest of people. You've always liked him.'

'I never thought of him as one of the family. What's he going to do after the war?'

'You'll have to ask him that yourself.'

There was no doubt that the war news was encouraging these days. Perhaps, Norma thought, perhaps Alan Edgerton would survive. May had no doubt about it. She went about the house, radiant, until at the end of the month Alan was posted. It all happened quite quickly and unexpectedly. He came to Castlemore to see them and tell them the news. They sat in the warm, comfortable sitting room, the rest of the world with all its unpleasantness shut out, and watched as May's expression froze on her face.

'Do you know where they're sending you?' Norma asked.

'No, ma'am, I don't, but I can guess.'

'Germany?'

'I wouldn't be surprised,' Alan agreed. 'It's a picnic over there now and if it weren't for Mary' (he never referred to her by the family name of May) 'I'd be glad to be in at the kill. It's going to be a triumphant progress, I'm certain of it.'

'When do you go?' Fiona asked.

'I leave in the morning.'

There was a silence, then Norma got up. 'Fiona and I will see about some supper for you. We'll leave you together. You'll have a lot to talk about. Supper in an hour?'

'Please don't bother, I'm not hungry.'

'Then help yourself to drinks and we'll have some coffee later.'

When they were left alone Alan took her hands and grinned at her.

'Hey, you look like we'd lost the war already. I'm not that bad a soldier.'

'It's no joke Alan. I'm scared.'

He put an arm round her and they sat silently. It was difficult to know what to say to her. He knew about Boy Loring and Edward Gentle, he knew what sort of war she had had. He felt tender and protective towards her, and he loved her quite genuinely. If he'd known they were going to send him away quite so quickly he might have let his proposal wait till he returned. What could he say to her? he wondered.

It was difficult for him. He'd fretted secretly during his time at Lochailort, watching the war pass him by. It wasn't that he was stupid or that he wanted to die or be wounded and maimed, but he had a zest for everything he did and he was fully trained. He was too much of a man to derive any real satisfaction from being an instructor in wartime. How could he explain to Mary that he was delighted to get this chance to take part in the mopping up of the doomed Third Reich? He was both eager to go and miserable at the prospect of leaving her now that he had found her. He remembered when he had first met her briefly in 1941, a young and tragic war widow. She had been remote then, and he had never dreamed that one day he'd marry her. It was odd how things worked out he thought.

Their silence lasted for a long time, for there were no words for them. If the war had taught people anything, surely the inadequacy of language was one of those things. In the frequent moments of truth which had become part of life itself, and not something you read about in a novel, people had begun to learn how to communicate in silence.

'I hope it won't be long,' she whispered a long time later when even the kissing had become meaningless.

'It can't be, honey. I mean it.'

'Don't catch any colds,' she whispered, using one of his favourite expressions.

'You know me.'

The trouble was that she did know him, had known him for a long time through remarks passed by his brother officers. He was almost the perfect commando – reckless yet cunning, fun-loving yet deadly. 'Mad as a hatter' one of them had called him, meaning it in a complimentary fashion. While he had been teaching other people how to kill silently in many ways, it hadn't mattered. Now, on the eve of his departure, it mattered a lot.

'Does your sister-in-law hear from Norman Windsor?' he asked, straightening his tie.

'Yes, yes she does. Quite often. He's in Belgium I believe.'

'We'll make it a double wedding, eh?' he suggested. 'They're serious, aren't they?'

'Yes.'

'Doesn't your mother mind?' It was easier to talk about other people.

'No, I don't think so. Alasdair's dead. Fiona can't spend her whole life in mourning.'

'You're right there, but your mother's a remarkable woman, isn't she?'

'She is,' May agreed.

'It must be quite a thing, coming from a house like this. How old is it?'

'Not much over a hundred years, though we haven't been in it that long. I think my great-grandfather bought it in 1853.'

'That's a long time. When we go to the States, aren't you going to miss this?'

She smiled at him. 'Of course I am, but I shan't mind. I've been away before. Besides, you might get a good job and then we could afford to come back for holidays.'

'Maybe. It must be funny, being a girl.'

'How do you mean?'

'Well, you fall in love with some guy and you marry him and you don't know where he's going to take you, what sort of house you'll live in, whether it will be baked beans or caviar. A girl like you, with a home like this, you take a hell of a chance.'

'What about you?'

'It's my life. I'm stuck with it. You're volunteering to join me, honey.'

'Alan, there's something I've never told you.'

'If it's about your past life, I don't want to know. We start clean, remember?'

'You don't understand, darling. I've got about twenty thousand dollars of my own, and when Mama dies, there will be a lot more.'

'My God, nobody told me. I didn't reckon you were broke, coming from a house like this, but twenty thousand?'

'Perhaps a bit more. I'm not taking too much of a chance – not financially. Just love me.'

'You stupid dame,' he said roughly. 'You think I don't love you?'

When Norma knocked later they were sitting chatting by the fire, quite relaxed. They'd said their goodbye. He stayed till almost midnight, and drank rather more of their whisky than he did usually. He kissed them all, and May saw him to his jeep. A few minutes later they heard it roar off along the drive and May went straight upstairs. Norma straightened a cushion idly and put the dirty glasses on a trolley where Ipla would find them in the morning.

'He's nice,' she remarked. 'Surely this time it will be all right?'

Fiona did not answer. She didn't want to tempt fate. She was thinking of Norman.

Alan wrote frequently, not very long letters but cheerful ones. He had gone almost directly to a commando unit and they were advancing across Europe – having a holiday, according to Alan. The end really was in sight and they held their breaths, the three women at Castlemore. On 29th April, 1945, the British crossed the River Elbe. Alan had no premonition of danger. It wasn't a war at all, just a very long route march in the direction of the main German forces. A lone sniper, knowing that he would soon be a prisoner or dead, sighted his rifle on a khaki target and fired.

'That's for my brother,' he muttered in German as he watched the man crumple.

It was a good shot, drilling a neat hole in Alan's forehead. He died with a look of surprise on his face which outdid the surprise on the face of the man next to him. There was almost no opposition, no firing. It was sheer, one hundred per cent filthy luck.

When the telegram was delivered to Castlemore, May and Fiona were out. They had taken the car into Fort William. Norma signed for it and opened it with no qualms. She read it, stone-faced, and the hall began to swim before her eyes. She did something very unusual. She drank a brandy in the middle of the morning. Fiona and May returned just before lunch and Norma beckoned Fiona to follow her upstairs.

It was obvious to Fiona that something was wrong, but what? Was it bad news, and if so what sort of bad news? Was it about Norman? Surely not. Norman had written to say that he was safe in Belgium doing some sort of staff job. Norma put her out of her misery as soon as they closed the door of her bedroom.

'Alan's dead,' she said. 'The telegram came while you were out. What are we going to do, Fiona?'

'Tell her,' Fiona answered, catching her breath. 'We can't keep it from her.'

'I know, but is there no way we can break it gently?'

'What?' Fiona demanded uncompromisingly. 'How can you hope to break that sort of news gently? You can't kill him off by instalments. What happened?'

'I don't know. It doesn't say. Read it for yourself.'

Fiona read the telegram and glanced at her grey-faced mother-in-law. Suddenly she remembered that Norma was over sixty. One took her so much for granted, she was so capable and so energetic, that often she seemed ageless. It was too bad.

'You'd better let me tell May,' she said impulsively, without the remotest idea of how she'd do it.

'Would you?' The question was an admission of defeat unusual from Norma.

'Of course. We're practically the same age and we've both lost husbands.'

'Yes,' Norma agreed quickly.

'Poor Norma.' Fiona kissed her. 'You suffer for all of us, don't you?'

'I'm a spoiled, pampered, wealthy old woman. Don't make a fuss of me,' Norma answered, turning away.

Fiona smiled at her and left the room. She walked down the big staircase which led into the hall, still holding the telegram in her hand. She'd never done this before, and anyway there was no book of rules. She caught a glimpse of May in the sitting room, rummaging among a pile of magazines. She went in and closed the door.

As May looked up, Fiona's arm went round her tightly. May looked startled. All Fiona knew was that it wasn't going to be like a scene from a war film. *'It's bad news darling.' 'You don't mean . . .' 'Yes.' 'Oh God no. Not dead.'* And so on, ad nauseam. There would be no dot-dots, as she called suspense scenes.

'Alan's dead,' she said coolly. 'The telegram came while we were out and Norma opened it.'

'*No!*' It was a scream. Fiona held her very tightly, and felt her sag against her arm.

'Yes, May.'

She wasted no words but held Mary close to her, held her with all her strength for May was struggling. At last May collapsed and her shoulders shook with deep heart-rending sobbing. Fiona led her to the sofa and sat beside her, holding her. It was a long time before May stopped crying. When she did, Fiona went and poured her a large brandy and handed it to her silently. May shook her head. She had picked up the telegram from the walnut coffee table where Fiona had put it, and she read it.

'I'll keep this,' she said dully and got up and left the room.

Fiona looked at the brandy, and with a shrug drank it herself. She was totally drained of energy. The worst of it was that she didn't know if she'd bungled it. It wasn't the sort of thing she could ask.

A few days later, on 8th May, the war in Europe ended officially. It was all over. The Americans were still fighting and dying in the Pacific, but the whole war effort would be turned on Japan now. It was the end. To the three women at Castlemore it was a cruel fate that had struck down Alan so near the end of the war. Fiona found it particularly difficult to talk to May about the end of the war, for, of course, peace meant that Norman was safe, that he would be coming back to her. Her own happiness seemed indecent in the face of May's tragic sufferings.

Neither May nor Fiona went to church often. Religion was not a subject much discussed at Castlemore. Like politics it was avoided generally. One could hardly ask May to go to church to offer thanks for the end of the war, but Norma did ask Fiona.

'Will you come with me?'

'Certainly, if you'd like me to.'

'Somehow I don't want to go alone this Sunday.'

Fiona understood. So often Norma did go alone. It would do her no harm to go with her this week, she thought. She was sceptical of organized religion, but she felt like saying 'thank you' to someone, so on Sunday 13th May they set out together, leaving May in her room. May seldom came downstairs before lunch nowadays.

The Episcopal Church was more crowded than usual this particular Sunday. The Reverend Duncan Mac-Intyre had chosen for the text of his sermon the words from the Lord's Prayer, 'For Thine is the Kingdom, the Power and the Glory.' He expounded his theme happily, speaking patriotically of the victory of God over evil, urging his flock that in this hour of triumph the credit should go to God. Norma, who generally found comfort in her religion, was oddly uncomforted this morning. Questions kept nagging at her mind as she looked round at the rest of the congregation. Was God on their side? Did God take sides at all in such un-Godly things as wars? Weren't Germans good Christians? She remembered once talking to her son, Alasdair, about the war and the causes of the war. Alasdair had remarkably clear views on the subject.

'Forget about the noble reasons for killing one another,' he had said in a rare moment of self-revelation. 'I remember having to read von Clausewitz. He said that war is the continuation of state policy by other means. Politicians chose war, Mama – it's a deliberate choice. I don't mean we chose it this time, but we're content to accept Hitler's choice. Our state policies clash, and war is the result. There's nothing noble about going to war. It's not at all like the knights of old rescuing damsels from dragons, if they ever did. It's just filthy politics, like everything else.'

There spoke a disillusioned soldier. Who was right, she wondered? Alasdair . . . or Duncan MacIntyre who wanted them to be careful to give all the credit and all the glory to God. Suddenly she realized that people were looking at her and she heard MacIntyre saying,

'Today we have with us the widow and the mother of one whose name is known to you all, whom many of us remember for happier days of peace – Colonel Alasdair MacInnes who won the Victoria Cross, only to die later, struck down by disease. I believe that if our hero were present in our midst he would tell us quite simply that the glory belongs to God and not to man, and that it is to God that we owe our safe deliverance.'

Norma exchanged a startled glance with Fiona. MacIntyre was fairly new to the district, but she found it difficult to believe that he could be guilty of such a breach of good taste as to refer to Alasdair, whom in fact he had

173

not known at all. She was angry, and two spots burned in her cheeks. Slowly they faded. The man was doing his job. What good would anger do?

Let God have the glory, she thought a little sadly. If He wants it, let Him have it. Nobody else in their right senses would have it as a free gift. The cruel memories of the past six years filled her for a moment, bringing tears to her eyes.

The Kingdom? The Power? The Glory?

Slowly her hand crept into Fiona's, and Fiona squeezed it gently. They sat together, two bewildered women, and allowed the man of God to finish his eulogy.

The transition from war to peace was disappointing. There was a moment of acute joy when they realized that it was all over and then they woke up a couple or mornings later and nothing seemed to have changed much. There was still rationing and austerity, the soldiers hadn't started to come home yet, and of course Japan was still fighting. In July people did begin to come home. First to arrive was Deirdre, now finished at Aberdeen University. She had her M.A. with honours, and Norma was proud of her. She would be going away again later in the year on a course, as she was determined to become an infant teacher, but for the moment she was safely home at Castlemore.

She and Fiona had already discussed Deirdre at some length, for she would be twenty-one on the 26th of November. They would like to give her a decent party, as good as rationing and restrictions would allow. One of the problems was whom to invite as so many people were away.

In the same month Maurice Blood returned from Washington for a long spell of leave before another appointment. He came to visit Norma one morning, on his own. He looked older now, with a touch of grey at his temples, and lines on his face which she had not seen before. He was a distinguished looking man and Norma thought that many women would find him attractive. It was not to be wondered at that he had found consolation in America for the separation from his wife.

'I came to thank you, Norma,' he said when they were alone.

'What on earth for, Maurice?'

'All you did of course, during that wretched un-pleasantness between Susan and myself. It's all right now.'

'I'm glad to hear that, believe me, but I did nothing. You know I didn't.'

'You mean that Susan wouldn't listen to you at first?' he smiled. 'I know that. She was wild with me for having written to you. Anyway the fact is that apparently you told her that she was a stupid woman.'

'Did she tell you that?'

'Yes, and what's more she took it to heart. I find her rather . . . contrite. Chastened is perhaps the word.'

'Don't give me too much credit, please, Maurice. I'm glad if things have improved.'

'Susan has rather fine qualities,' he said unexpectedly. 'One doesn't always notice them. You see unfortunately her father left her with a terrible inferiority complex. She married me for my title you know – and the money she thought I had. Of course I haven't nearly enough money to satisfy her. She was quite frank about it. She never pretended she loved me at the time of our wedding. I hoped that would follow.'

'I had no idea. What made you marry her?'

'I loved her,' he said quietly. 'It was as simple as that. She's been a good wife in many ways. I know she's pre-tentious and snobbish, sometimes a little ridiculous, but that's only one side of the story.'

'I see. I'm glad you see her in that light. I was afraid the marriage was going to end with you splitting up.'

'It has in a way, with this job of mine,' he laughed.

'Are you going abroad again?'

'Oh yes, at the end of the year. I've got an embassy at last – Stockholm. It's a very unexpected promotion.'

'Will Susan go with you?'

'No, she doesn't want to. Perhaps it's better if she stays at home. She and the boys will come out for holidays. Vernon goes to Eton this year, you see.'

'Susan told me. You're going to be separated again?'

'For a few more years, but not so absolutely as we were while I was in the United States. As I say, there will be holidays.'

'So long as you're satisfied.'

'I'm not entirely, but it's an improvement. I shall probably retire after this appointment. I fancy settling at Grunaglack. I think I could make some money out of it if I buy some good land. I shall study farming and forestry in my spare time. Ambassadors do have spare time, you know.'

'It will be better for the family if you are at home.'

'Yes,' he agreed. 'Meantime I'm stuck with Stockholm. I had to accept. I'll be getting my K.C.M.G. in the New Year's Honours List. It goes with the job.'

'Congratulations.'

He smiled. 'Thank you. It's always pleasing to know one has satisfied one's masters. Now I really wanted to ask you about May.'

Norma's expression changed. 'Yes?'

'Susan has told me all about her. Norma, do you think she'd like to come to Stockholm with me for a few months, or a year or two? It would make a change for her.'

'Do you mean to stay at the Embassy?'

'Yes. It is usual for an Ambassador's wife to accompany him, to be his hostess. It will be a little awkward for me without Susan; in fact in the good old days I'd not have been allowed to go alone. It seemed to me that May could be hostess for me for a time. It would make a change for her, take her mind off things.'

'If she'll go, it's a splendid idea. Would you like me to speak to her?'

'Why not let me do so?'

'If you'd rather. She's upstairs in her room. She spends hours there nowadays.'

'I'm not terribly surprised. It's been a pretty awful business. Perhaps you could ask her to come down and see me.'

Norma nodded, bewildered at the speed of it all. She went up to May and a few minutes later May came into the room alone. Maurice chatted to her pleasantly for a while, putting her at ease. Once or twice he even managed to evoke a brief smile. Then he asked her if she would like to come to Stockholm and explained his predicament.

'I can't take Susan's place,' she said automatically.

'No, but it would be a tremendous help to me at the beginning if I had someone to deal with the entertaining. It would be a holiday for you. You can stay for as short a time as you please.'

It did not occur to her to ask how he had managed in Washington without a wife. Maurice could have managed very easily without her, although it was true that she would be a help to him. He was sorry for her and he wanted to help, but he did not want to do it too obviously in case she rejected him.

They talked about it for half an hour and May agreed to think about it. He assured her that there was no hurry. He knew that she would probably come as he could see that the idea appealed to her. It would be such a complete change.

Before the summer ended, Sir Lauchlan came home from London. He had accumulated a lot of leave and had insisted on having it now that the war was over.

'What happens next?' Leona asked him the day after he had arrived at Ardclune.

'I don't know. They wanted me to go back to India, but I refused.'

'Why, darling?'

'Because India is going to get its independence. I don't want to go back now. It will be totally different from the India we both knew. They weren't very pleased with me.'

'Why not?'

'They do like you to be co-operative,' he laughed. 'Have you forgotten?'

'No, dear.'

'They talked of promotion and I talked of leave. I think I've blotted my copybook. They're going to let me know, which probably means I'll be landed with some sort of grubby desk job in London.'

'Must you take it?'

'No, but I think I ought to hang on for a few years. Besides, I may get the chance to do something useful one day. I don't feel very much of a success. A lot of early promise has gone to waste.'

'What do I care about success?' Leona asked, kissing him.

'You're the very finest wife any man ever had. You'd put up with me if I were a tramp.'

'You're such a wonderful tramp, darling.'

'I'm flattered. Meantime I've got four months at home, think of it.'

'How did you manage that?'

'It's a bit of a swindle really, but I'm actually entitled to it, so I insisted on having it.'

'Bless you,' she laughed.

'I've seen so little of you. I know ours hasn't been a tragic war, as it was at Castlemore, but years of separation are no joke. I hardly know Eve and Mary.'

'Mary goes to boarding school this year.'

'I know. They're growing up too quickly for me. Most of all, I feel a stranger with you.'

'You didn't act like one last night,' she answered, her eyes sparkling.

'You know very well what I mean. Let's enjoy the country for a few months, let's get to know each other again, because it will be Christmas in London for us unless I'm mistaken.'

'I don't care where it is, as long as we're together,' she sighed happily. 'Incidentally, darling, you'll be at home for Deirdre's twenty-first birthday – just.'

'When is it?'

'The 26th of November. Norma is trying to organize some sort of proper party for her.'

'We must buy her something nice for the occasion. How is Deirdre anyway?'

'She got an honours M.A. at Aberdeen. She's turning out very well, as well as being a beauty.'

'Is she? I look forward to seeing her. Come, let's go for a stroll.'

'Finvola won't want me to leave,' Leona said as they left the house.

'That's a pity, but I think I have some right to your company.'

'I know, darling, but she'll be all alone. She raised the subject a few days ago, before you came back. She wants us to come to live here. In fact, she seems to think that although Daddy left the house to her, it is as much ours as hers and that we shouldn't look on it as hers alone.'

'That's extraordinarily nice of her. She must have mellowed a lot. I'd planned to do a few more years in the Service, say till 1953. I'd like to get out when I'm fifty and have some pleasure in life before they bury me.'

'You'll live to be a hundred, you're so strong.'

'So much the better. I've been wondering what to do when I retire. It would be nice to have this place to come to. I've always liked it. Perhaps we could spend holidays with Finvola each year, in the summer. I wouldn't like her to be too lonely.'

'You're a thoughtful man.'

'Let's be honest,' he laughed. 'At the moment I'm thinking mostly of myself. I want you, Aline Iona MacInnes. You follow me, I hope?'

'Anywhere, darling. Lot's wife, that's me.'

They smiled happily at one another.

At the end of the summer the various children went off to their schools, Vernon to Eton, Eve and Mary to Miss Weir's, Philip to his preparatory school. Only Pal Al and Frances Mary went to school locally, and came home to Castlemore every evening. Norma became more preoccupied with the question of Deirdre's party and everyone was involved whether they wanted it or not. May had agreed to go to Stockholm with Lord Maurice in January, and already she seemed more cheerful, less withdrawn and silent.

For Fiona the waiting was heartbreak. Norman was in Paris, and wrote every week. It was ridiculous that now the war was over they should still be apart like this, and she wished they would get a move on and release him from the Army and send him back. They were not officially engaged, they were saving that for his return, and their letters were full of their plans.

Deirdre's birthday fell on a Monday, so they held the party two days before, on the Saturday. She was attending a course near Edinburgh and the friends from university whom she had asked Norma to invite were also either working or still at university, so it had to be the week-end. It was the first big family function at Castlemore for a long time, and Norma had dug out the fairy lights and coloured spotlights that they had used before the war to illuminate the front of the house in the evenings when there was a dance or party, and there had been a general round-up of food and drink. Considering the circumstances it was a very respectable buffet indeed.

Susan had surprised them by producing quite a number of things from her private hoard, including six cases of good champagne.

It was quite a family gathering. At Castlemore were Deirdre, Norma, Fiona and May, and the children Pal Al and Frances Mary had been allowed to stay up late. Susan and Maurice came up from Grunaglack, and Leona and Rajah brought Finvola along from Ardclune. There were local friends of the family, and there were half a dozen or so of Deirdre's friends from Aberdeen. Altogether there were thirty people.

Deirdre, who had arrived home on the afternoon of the party, had no idea how much trouble had been taken. She had a lovely new evening dress as the result of a family effort in donating clothing coupons. Most of the others had their evening dress from before the war. One could almost have imagined that it was a proper pre-war party. They danced to records, and the champagne disguised the shortage of whisky, brandy and other drinks.

It was only a pity, Norma felt, that there were no young men Deirdre's age. The three she had invited had paired off with the three girls she had invited. Deirdre did not seem to mind this, and certainly it did not prevent her from dancing every dance. It was typical of dances held at that time that there were more women than men. The effects of the war were still manifest in so many ways.

Rajah saw Norma standing in a corner by herself, watching the dancers. It was almost midnight. He came and joined her.

'Satisfied?' he asked.

'I think it isn't too bad. Fiona and May did a wonderful job of decorating.'

'They did. I always think this hall looks so nice when there's a dance.'

'I know,' she agreed, pleased. 'In many ways I feel it is the nicest room in the house. We used to use it a lot when I first came here.'

'Yes, I daresay you did. Deirdre is radiant tonight.'

'Isn't she? Perhaps now that the war's over she'll meet some nice young man.'

'You're a matchmaker,' he accused.

'Where she's concerned, yes. I want to see her settled. I'm very fond of her.'

'You're fond of us all, aren't you? Fiona looks a little sad.'

'That's natural, Rajah. She is waiting for Norman Windsor to come back. If he could have been here to-night it would have been just perfect.'

'Nothing is ever perfect, is it? Still, we get close to it sometimes,' he added, looking all round and noticing his own wife who seemed more lovely than ever. 'Come and dance with me,' he invited.

'Why not dance with someone younger?' she answered. 'You don't want to bother about an old grandmother like me.'

'That's where you're wrong. You aren't old at all. You're not going to turn me down are you?'

'You've a glib tongue,' she chided, but she accepted his invitation happily.

It was two o'clock when the last of the guests who were not staying at Castlemore departed. Before she went up to her room Deirdre kissed her aunt.

'It was wonderful. You make me ashamed. I don't deserve it.'

'What a silly child you are. I wonder why we bothered to send you to university. Of course you deserve it. I'm glad you liked it.'

'Oh Aunt Norma, I wish I could tell you.'

Norma watched her run upstairs and then with a little smile followed more slowly. Cleaning up could wait.

It was early next morning when Fiona awakened. She put on her dressing gown and went downstairs. Somehow everything looked a little sad in the morning light. It would take the best part of an hour to clear up the mess. She went to the windows and looked out at the grounds, at the fountain and the summer house, at the bare flower beds, at the dripping trees, for it had rained in the night. The loch was sullen and dull.

All parties come to an end, she thought. It was a pity. This wet Sunday morning in November was the very epitome of mornings-after. Suddenly she saw a bicycle wobbling along the drive towards the house. She could not make out who was on it, and she wondered who could be calling at eight o'clock on a Sunday morning. As the cycle reached the front of the house she realized that the dark-suited cyclist was vaguely familiar. She unlocked the doors and opened them as he came up the steps. He smiled at her.

'Good morning, Mistress MacInnes.'

'Mr Thompson. What are you doing here?' It was the local postman.

'I was passing and I thought I'd bring this. It's a letter – for you as it happens. It must have got caught up in my satchel and I discovered it at home yesterday evening. You see I don't go back to the post office on a Saturday at lunchtime. I take the satchel home.'

'Thank you very much.'

'I'm sorry for the delay. It's a Forces letter so I thought you'd want it now, and not be waiting till tomorrow morning. I was on my way to my sister's house and I thought I'd drop it off.'

It would be from Norman, she thought with delight.

'That's very kind of you, Mr Thompson. Thank you very much.'

'Don't thank me. It's my fault you didn't get the letter yesterday. I can't think how such a thing could have happened. It's never happened before. Well, good morning.'

'Good morning.'

She smiled as he went down to his bicycle, and waved as he trundled off. Then she shut the door and slit open the envelope. She scanned the letter quickly, and her face broke into a broad smile.

It was all right at last. Norman was coming home.